LOVE & OTHER GAMES

Book 2 in The Professional Players Series

LYNDSEY GALLAGHER

CHAPTER ONE

EMMA

As I pace the varnished wooden floor of my new extension, I'm overcome with a sinking suspicion that I'm about to become single once again. There's no sign of Paul, and our taxi is due to arrive in ten minutes. I've called him five times. Desperate, you may say, and I'd completely agree.

I'm an expert at the unwritten rules of dating, and repeated phone calls are solidly up there with 'don't mention your ex' and 'never have sex on the first date.' I rarely make an exception to any rule, but today we have a plane to catch. I'm not prepared to miss the flight to Croatia for Abby and Callum's wedding.

Several scenarios flit through my mind as to why Paul isn't currently standing at my front door with his luggage. Perhaps he's been involved in a traffic accident? Or maybe a gang of delinquent teenagers mugged him for drug money while he was on his way?

My rose gold sandals thwack against the floor. Pacing is a bad habit, but at least it gets my daily steps in. However, it doesn't do anything to eradicate the niggle of worry that warns me I've done it again; come on too strong, scared yet another one away. I have no problem attracting men, but even with strict adherence to the unwritten rules, I just can't seem to keep them. The second I let my guard down, the second I get even a tiny bit comfortable and *dare* to admit that I'm looking for something serious, I'm dumped right back at square one.

The familiar bars of Beyonce's 'Single Ladies' erupt from my phone, startling the silence. My little sister Holly picked my ringtone. In her mind being single is something to celebrate. Where I have spent most of my adult life looking for my one true love, Holly is content looking for lots of love. But she has youth on her side, and being the youngest of three girls – zero family pressure. I'm looking for husband material, and not just because of my emotionally challenged mother's repetitive digs regarding my inability to bag one, and my ever-shrinking ovaries.

I tap the green icon and press the phone tightly to my ear. 'Paul, is everything okay?'

'Emma. I'm not going to make it.'

I knew it. Deep down, I knew this would happen. His absence has already spoken volumes.

'Why?' My heart lurches in my chest.

'I'm stuck at work. The deal we're trying to negotiate isn't going as smoothly as I'd hoped.'

'So you'll meet me at the airport instead?' I hate the uncertainty that creeps into my tone.

'No. I won't make the holiday. The wedding.' He clears his throat, and the silence that follows is uncomfortable.

'You are joking?'

'I'm deadly serious, Emma. This client is a big deal to me. If I don't nail things down this weekend, another agency could swoop in and steal the deal from underneath my nose.

You know how it is, babe.' His patronising tone ignites a suppressed fire flickering in the depth of my abdomen.

'This wedding is a big deal to me, Paul. I really wanted you to be there.' Swallowing down my irritation, I wait with bated breath to see if he might miraculously have a change of heart.

Silence from the other end of the phone. He's probably staring into his computer screen, waiting to get the predictable bollocking over with.

Maybe it's weddings, in general, he tries to avoid? If that's the case, he's going to be no good to me, because I want the works; the embarrassingly humungous white dress, the Cathedral overflowing with guests, 'Pachelbel's Canon' belting out from the organ.

'You wanted *me* to go to the wedding? Or you wanted *someone* to go as your date to the wedding?' Paul asks, a knowing arrogance weaves into his tone.

Huh. I can't believe he's trying to turn this around on me! Though...perhaps he has a point. For the previous few weeks, I've been ignoring that niggling inner inkling that perhaps we aren't entirely compatible, brushing it off, squashing it down. The air whooshes out of my chest at the worrying prospect of starting over again; scrolling thousands of meaningless faces, desperately searching for one that might demonstrate some sort of potential. Embarking on endless disastrous dates in the hope of eventually finding my very own Prince Charming.

Paul clears his throat. 'This isn't working, Emma. Your need to get a ring on *that* finger is painful. Life isn't like one of those crappy romance novels you read. You're a beautiful girl, even without the inch-thick make-up, but your desperation makes you ugly.'

His comments rip through me, tearing me up from the inside out, twisting my intestines around my heart and temporarily winding me. My mouth moves, but no sound comes out.

What's wrong with wanting to get married? It's a normal ritual in society. And in the absence of it actually happening in real life, what's wrong with seeking solace in a bit of fictional romance?

Ten seconds pass silently while I gather the strength to end this conversation with my dignity intact, no mean feat when he's just scraped the top of a deeply etched wound. Frankie, my boxer puppy, stands at my feet protectively. His black eyes remain fixed on me, head cocked in concern. I rub his silky ear between my finger and thumb affectionately.

'You are right, Paul. This isn't working. I wish you all the best. I really do.' I force the words out of my mouth and disconnect the call.

'Another one bites the dust, Frankie. Six more months of my life wasted with the wrong man. Perhaps we are destined to be just the two of us?'

Frankie wags his tail and follows me into the lounge where I gather my luggage.

Though the relationship was more likely to lead me down the garden path than up the aisle, its inevitable end, and yet another rejection, stings.

Holly calls me Emma The Assassin because she swears I'm cutthroat. In or out. Do or die. She might be right when it comes to business, but when it comes to men she is sadly very wrong. Someone with transferable skills wouldn't be considering adopting four cats and joining the local crochet club. If I was any good at dating, I wouldn't have to be doing it at all, I'd be sitting at home binge-watching Netflix, with my charming, loyal husband, while our adorable children slept quietly upstairs.

Holly claims that when I meet a man who demonstrates potential, I do this weird nail thrumming on whatever hard surface is available, be it a sticky bar top in an over-priced wine bar, the roof of a stationary car, or even once on the side of the kitchen tea caddy as I interrogated the architect planning the extension at the back of my house.

The finger tapping translates as my own private Morse code as I mentally list the subject's positive versus negative traits and potential suitability. It's kind of crazy, but it's subconscious. I'm not even aware that I'm doing it. Luckily for me, very few people have cracked the code. Only one, in fact, and thankfully that's my baby sister, who is one of my best friends and most trusted confidants.

Holly swears blind that if the beat sounds regular and solid, like 'We Will Rock You', they're in with a fighting chance. (The architect turned out to be gay, no amount of thrumming was going to change that. I was at the peak of Queen's famous resounding chorus before he less than subtly dropped in his boyfriend has a penchant for Pina Coladas and bottomless brunches).

If the tapping beat is faster, more impatient, it's already a resounding no. They're dismissed before they've had the opportunity to swipe right.

Another heartfelt sigh escapes my lips, but honestly, I'm far from distraught. Disappointed, but not distraught. I file Paul's comments amongst the murkiest parts of my brain to analyse and agonise over when sleep alludes me, unable to dwell on my latest failure at this precise moment. Though I am now dateless – I still have a plane to catch.

Hastily, I check I have everything; keys, phone, purse, passport, book, all tucked securely into my favourite Prada crossover satchel. Taking one last glance at my reflection, I use my new sunglasses as a hairband to tame my waist-length free-falling locks.

Make-up was my first true love; the bright popping coloured lip shades, the glittering palates, promising glamour and sparkle. My own is immaculate. It has to be because it's my armour, my shield against the world. It gives me the confidence to pose as the successful businesswoman most people believe me to be. Doublewear foundation covers a magnitude of sins; skin pigmentation, an unhealthy sugar addiction, and my infuriating inability to get more than five hours sleep.

Beyonce's 'Single Ladies' pierces the air again. For a second, I wonder if it's Paul, if he's changed his mind. Too late, the damage is done, and I'm not one for giving second chances. A quick glance at the screen shows it's Sarah, the girl I entrust to manage my business empire for me in my absence.

'Emma, sorry to bother you when you are on holiday.' Sarah's tone is apologetic. She is my longest-standing employee and a good friend at this stage too.

'Ring me anytime. What's up?'

'It's not good news, I'm afraid. The solicitor has been in touch. There's been another bid on the Balbriggan property.' She pauses while I digest this disheartening snippet of information.

This is my new venture, my latest business baby; a luxury spa, which will provide a brand-new flagship, marking my fifth branch of Believe in Beauty in as many years. It's also heavily entwined with my newest and most costly investment so far.

'How much?' I hold my breath in anticipation.

'1.1 million euro.'

'Shit.' A low whistle rolls from my lips. 'Ring the accountant, see what we can realistically stretch to. If this goes into a full-on bidding war, we need to be prepared. I cannot lose this property. It stands for too much.'

'Okay. I'll be in touch.' Sarah hangs up.

The low thrum of an engine outside signals the arrival of my taxi. I kiss Frankie goodbye and promise him my mother will be along to collect him shortly. She might be devoid of emotion when it comes to her middle daughter, but I reluctantly entrust her with my adorable fur baby, the most loyal creature on this planet.

Stepping out into the September sunshine, I pull my sunglasses from my head and slide into the backseat. The driver lifts my luggage into the boot, no mean feat considering it's crammed with ten shades of lipstick, fifteen dresses, six bikinis and a variety of wedges, sandals and stilettos. One can never be too prepared.

'Which terminal, pet?' The driver's voice is gentle, fatherly, reminding me of my own dad, who works out of the country more often than he is in it, no doubt chased away by my mother's coldness or indifference.

'South, please.' I run my fingers over the soft fabric of my maxi dress and try not to think about Paul's parting comments. Will he go back to banging Tammy-tits, his busty twenty-two-year-old PA? He assured me it was over long before he met me, but one look at her informed me she still had designs on him. Surprisingly, I don't care either way.

Dublin airport is only ten minutes away from my red brick house in Swords, and traffic is light. As the car passes the familiar landmarks, my thoughts turn to Abby and her upcoming nuptials. She's a radio presenter – the wedding will be full of Irish celebrities. Not only did she snag one of Ireland's most handsome rugby players, but they also have a beautiful five-month-old daughter, Casey. I don't begrudge her, on the contrary, she deserves every happiness, having had rotten luck in the past. But I can't help but wonder if I haven't had enough rotten luck now too? How many more frogs will I have to kiss before I find my prince?

I huff unwittingly, and the taxi driver glances back in his rearview mirror.

'You alright back there, pet?' His unexpected kindness

results in tears brimming, threatening to spill all over my painstakingly applied make-up. I swallow hard, pushing them back in place.

'Grand, thanks.' I lie. I need to pull myself together. I'm going on holiday. To witness the nuptials of one of my closest friends. I won't let Paul's parting remarks or anything else ruin it.

As the view of the city fades behind us, I contemplate how and when I will resume the husband search. If it's not Tinder, it will be back to scouring trendy cocktail bars on a Friday night. Serial dating is exhausting. When I was younger, I enjoyed it, filled with misplaced hope every single time I went on a new date. Each date offered a chance, an opportunity. After an epic amount of time wasters and appalling experiences, the prospect now seems worse than manual labour in forty-degree heat.

Shrinking ovaries aside, perhaps a lifetime of watching *Don't Tell the Bride* alone isn't the worst thing in the world? At least I won't have to share the remote. Imagine lying on the sofa in my pyjamas on a Friday night, eating whichever takeaway I choose, make-up free and bra-less. Though it doesn't even have to be a lifetime...even a few months would be an absolute treat.

The thought of a reprieve from the romantic rat race is overwhelmingly appealing, but the fact is, I'm not getting any younger.

Removing my phone from the satchel, I glare at the little square apps; Tinder, Hinge and Plenty of Fish. Deep down inside, I know that my heart and head can't take much more rejection. Not at this point anyway. I'm indifferent about Paul. It was the one before him that cut me the deepest. I have a tendency to jump from one man to another, almost frightened to be alone, trapped in my eternal quest of finding a man to settle down with.

Would a couple of months make that much difference in the real scheme of things?

In a moment of quick decision, I delete all the dating apps from my phone. Maybe I am cutthroat after all? If I take myself out of the game, I can't lose. An instant surge of relief ripples through me. Flicking my hair back from my face with a single-minded determination, I decide to devote my attention solely to the spa for the next three months. It might not keep me warm at night, but it will keep me busy. Business is the one thing that I excel at, so it's immeasurably safer to invest in, than risky gambles with matters of the heart. A three-month break will do me the world of good; recharge, reassess and restart from a stronger position.

Arriving at the airport with a newfound spring in my step, I pay the driver, humming away to myself, lighter than I've been in months.

CHAPTER TWO

EDDIE

I'm late as usual, I can't help it. It's one of my world-renowned failings. I shouldn't have gone out last night, but I needed a distraction from my latest, and most epic, bust up with Maria. She's hot, cold, hot, cold. It's finally over, and frankly, I'm glad to be shot of her mental games.

With Balbriggan beach only eight metres behind me, I inhale the familiar salt and seaweed scent as the waves of the Irish Sea crash against the shore. Dublin is sunny but breezy today, with that distinct nip in the air, the one that creeps in every year when kids start back at school.

I cross the narrow road and lean on the high bricked wall to wait for the estate agent. I'm not the only one that's late this morning. A man in his forties pulls up in a black Volvo. He hurriedly exits his car, smoothing down his crumpled suit and wipes his hand on his jacket before reaching out to shake mine.

'Eddie Harrington?' He checks, although by the awestruck

way he's staring at me, he already knows who I am. 'It's a pleasure to meet you. I'm Tim O'Rourke, the agent charged with selling this property.'

'Tim, I don't mean to be a dick, but I'm in a massive rush today. It's Callum Connolly's wedding in four days, and I have a plane to catch. Can we make this quick? I'll make it easy for you. I'm ninety-nine per cent sure I'm going to purchase this property for my brother. So if we could just have a quick look inside, I'll get a formal offer sent across to you from my solicitor before I board my flight.' I'd already viewed five others, all of which claimed to have a sea view, which might be true if you stood on the kitchen table, jumped up and down in the air and craned your neck. When this place suddenly came to auction, it felt like fate.

'Great. Wonderful. Though the bidding is technically open until Tuesday, and there is a lot of interest. Properties such as this rarely come up for auction. But I'm sure we can arrange something.' Tim gives me a conspiring 'boys together' type of wink, and I have to fight my eyes from rolling in my head.

He pulls out the key from his trouser pocket and unlocks the door with shaky fingers. Following him into a spacious corridor, I note the stairs are wide enough to fit a stairlift. The house is very similar to the one I live in myself, five doors down. Having bought that property fifteen months ago, I then spent the first nine months renovating. It's the ultimate bachelor pad with a bar area, a games room, thick carpets, expensive decor, and enormous triple-glazed windows which open out on to a sea-facing balcony. I haven't put a hot tub in yet, but it's on the to-do list. The fact of the matter is that I'm away training more often than I'm in it at the moment.

'How's the rugby going?' Tim interrupts my thoughts,

determined to make conversation despite my aforementioned time constraints.

'Grand thanks. If I'm successful with this property, I'll send you two match tickets to a home game.' It's a sneaky bribe. Anything to seal the deal.

I take in the double doors, high ceilings and wide corridors. It will be perfect for my brother and his family when they relocate from the States next month. He heavily relies on the use of a wheelchair, and the back garden is completely paved. Another bonus – minimal maintenance will be required. Opening the sliding doors, I'm greeted by the rhythmic sound of the waves again. I hope the seaside location will soften the blow for Matthew, sweeten the fact that he has no choice but to return home.

'I'll take it,' I tell Tim, retracing my steps out to the front door.

'Don't you want to know what the current bid is?' A frown burrows on Tim's bushy eyebrows.

'My solicitor will deal with everything. She'll be in touch with a formal offer within the hour.' She's actually my older sister. Keira takes care of all of my finances, but Tim doesn't need to know that.

'The auction closes on Tuesday morning at ten a.m. The highest bidder must be available to sign the paperwork that day. This property *is* in great demand,' he repeats.

They all say that, though, don't they? It's a direct quote from The Salesman's Handbook.

'I'll send you those match tickets.' I couldn't be any more obvious, but I don't care. The property is perfect for Matthew. I have to have it.

I jump into the taxi that awaits me, five doors down. The driver chews noisily on a piece of gum as we begin the journey to Dublin airport.

My mind drifts to Matthew again – he's never far from my

thoughts. He will hate me for buying him a house. He will assume it's guilt. Maybe it is, but we all want to ensure his transition back to Ireland goes as smoothly as possible. I'll find a company that manufactures stairlifts and get one fitted the second I sign that contract.

An accident on the motorway adds forty-five minutes to the journey. I throw the driver a fifty, grab my holdall and rush towards the Aer Lingus check-in desk.

'Dubrovnik.' I tell the twenty-something girl, clothed head to toe in the familiar shade of green.

'Cutting it fine.' She observes with a raised eyebrow. If she recognises me as the Irish rugby team's current hooker, she doesn't show it.

I leg it towards security, skidding to an abrupt halt at the back of a long line of unmoving holidaymakers. What is the hold-up? I glance at my watch pointedly and bite back the 'for fuck's sake' that's on the tip of my tongue. If we don't get moving soon, there's an acute possibility that I might miss the flight to one of my best friends' wedding. My size twelve Nikes tap against the dirty floor impatiently, for all the fucking good it does me.

A woman's outraged voice travels the length of the queue. I can't make out a word that she's saying, but the passengers in front of me are nudging one another and sniggering. I side-step to get a better look.

A tall, curvaceous brunette stands with her back to me, berating two guards, who are currently rifling through her small suitcase. She flicks her long dark hair aggressively with the back of her hand, and her tanned arms fly frantically around in exaggerated gestures. Dresses line the metal surfaces. Brightly coloured bikinis and numerous lone shoes are strewn across the floor. Whatever the security guys are looking for, they haven't found it yet. If her case is over-weight, I'll happily pay the difference for her trouble, if she'd just get the fuck on with it and quit holding everyone up. I debate calling out to her with my offer.

The woman's tone becomes increasingly irate as a black lace bra drops to the floor. I'm temporarily distracted from my own concerns, entranced by her picture-perfect hourglass figure captured in a slim-fitting, floor-length dress.

After what feels like an eternity, the brunette locates what she's been looking for. She triumphantly thrusts a flashing, vibrating electric toothbrush in the guard's face and tilts her head defiantly. His shoulders sag, and his reddening face drops to the floor.

I can't help it. An explosive rumbling laugh erupts from the depth of my gut as I realise the extent of the situation. The brunette spins swiftly round on her heel to locate the source of the amusement. Her glinting emerald glare penetrates me like a bullet. My laughter lodges in my windpipe as I absorb her familiar features; it's Emma.

Now it's me that looks to the floor, though I raise one arm casually in a greeting which I hope conveys I'm apologetic and not just for laughing at her current misfortune. I haven't seen her since *that* night. Or morning, should I say. That's not to say I haven't thought about her, though. Quite the contrary, in fact.

The line moves again. I remove my belt and shoes in preparation for the metal detector, keeping my eyes fully focussed on Emma's rapidly disappearing silhouette. Obviously, she's going to Callum and Abby's wedding.

I have tried so hard not to think about what happened last year, about what might have been, but if I'm brutally honest, she's never far from my mind. For a split second, I imagine the two of us travelling together, like the couple everyone was so sure we'd become. But like everything else in my life, I fucked it up.

I breeze through security with a nod of acknowledgement

from the two guards, who are clearly in no doubt about who I am. I scan the televisions for directions to my gate and jog towards it, slinging my holdall over my shoulder. I wonder if I'll be anywhere near Emma? If her glare was anything to go on, it's probably safer if I'm not.

CHAPTER THREE

EMMA

Dragging my case towards the gate, I pretend not to care that *The One That Got Away* is on my flight. I cringe remembering how quickly I'd dropped my three-date rule for him, along with my mismatched underwear. When it comes to the wrong men, I've had them all. Except I never really did have him, of course...unless you count that one tiny *sensational* night, that I've bitterly regretted ever since. I had hoped to wave my stockbroker boyfriend under his nose, but clearly, I can't even do that now.

Eddie Harrington, friend of the groom and Callum's former teammate, used me. Which I wouldn't even have been entirely averse to if he'd been honest about the situation. But he tricked me with declarations like 'Holy fuck I never thought I'd meet someone like you', 'You are rocking my world', and my all-time favourite, 'What are you doing for the rest of your life?' I know, I know, at my age and with my dating history, I really should have known better than to fall at the feet of Ireland's most alluring rugby player.

Huffing like a hormonal teenager, I step onto the Aer Lingus flight with only minutes to spare. He's probably only thirty seconds behind me, with his French girlfriend and former tennis player, Maria Vaillancourt, in tow. Abby calls her Maria Likes-To-Snort, due to the substantial amount of cocaine found in her room at Wimbledon earlier in the year. She claimed it was planted, but we'll never know because she retired immediately afterwards due to an 'ongoing injury', thereby escaping the blood tests. According to the tabloids, she's since opened a tennis academy for teenagers in her hometown on the outskirts of Paris.

Most of the passengers are already on board thanks to those two eejits searching for a vibrator I hadn't packed, funnily enough. Though if I knew Hooker Harrington would be in such close proximity, maybe I should have.

I hand my boarding pass to the stewardess, and she points me to an aisle seat on the left, eight rows back. The window seat next to mine is empty. Thank god. In fact, the entire row is empty; fingers crossed it stays that way. I slide into my seat and force my bulging travel case under the chair in front of me.

A family of four board the plane noisily, and the air hostess points them in my direction. The little boy races towards me wearing an inflatable ring and a batman hat. The girl wears a swimming costume over cerise leggings and clings to her mother's calves, wailing. I glance at the free seat next to me and the two free seats across the aisle, realising I will separate this family if I stay where I am.

The dad places their luggage in the cabin above my head and looks around uncertainly, considering their predicament.

'Do you want me to swap with you?' The words are out of my mouth before I stop to consider them. Relief etches onto the lines of the tired mother's face as she realises she won't have to battle the toddlers alone.

'Would you mind?' Both parents say in unison, estranged members of *The Brady Bunch*. I watch as they exchange an entire conversation in one shared glance. How I envy them that ability, their security and familiarity. All I've ever wanted is a normal family.

'Not at all.' I tug my suitcase out again and stoop as I shuffle clumsily from my seat.

'My seat is in row thirteen. Unlucky for some, but not us. Thanks to you.' The dad points me to my new aisle seat, five rows further back. It's a good job I'm not superstitious, because I already hate flying. I hope this seat's not unlucky for me, reminding myself that if the plane goes down, no matter which seat we occupy, we're all equally doomed.

I nod politely at several other passengers as I pass by. The cabin crew announcement resonates over the speaker as the safety demonstration begins. I fight to haul my heavy case into the tiny locker above, but it refuses to submit easily.

'Can I help you with that?' A rich, gravelly voice interrupts my thoughts from behind. I jump, startled more at the proximity of another person rather than the voice. My head twists to the side in horror as I realise who my new travel companion is.

'You? Huh.' That's my reward for doing a good deed. Thirteen is certainly proving unlucky for me. Now I'll have to sit next to him while he paws all over Maria, merely millimetres away from me. Fuck my life. Maybe the plane crashing wouldn't be the worst thing in the world.

'I'm afraid so.' Eddie gazes at me with enormous espresso-coloured eyes. They aren't a million miles away from the shade of Frankie's, only Frankie's exude a great deal more sincerity.

That face is the one I have been seeing in my dreams for almost a year now. Far from symmetrical, his nose is very slightly crooked from a break, likely received on the pitch.

Instead of taking away from his looks, it provides character. A small silvery scar sits, indented into his left cheekbone. Despite this, he somehow still manages to pull off the pretty boy look.

I stand aside, allowing him to wedge my case into the tight space, seeing as he is five inches taller than me. It's the least he can do after the way he treated me. No, that's unfair. I'm a big girl; I knew what I was doing. Stupidly, I just thought I was different. That we were different. The realisation that I wasn't, and that there was no 'we' was crippling. I glance towards the exit doors that the stewardess is slamming shut and securing. Where is Maria?

Slipping into my seat, I hold my knees to the side, allowing him to squeeze past and position himself in the window seat. As his legs brush mine, I hold my breath to stop myself panting in his presence. Huge shoulders might be advantageous for a rugby player, not quite so beneficial squashed in the tight confines of an aeroplane with a woman you shagged, and shagged off.

His arm falls companionably on the rest against mine. Our thighs touch, leaning against each other inescapably. Prickling tingles ripple the skin of my legs. I'm relieved I wore something full length, hiding the effect he still manages to create.

I pull out my phone and send Holly a text before I have to turn it off.

Hooker Harrington next to me on the plane. Help!!

Her reply is instantaneous.

Swap seats with Paul.

I reply, tilting my phone in the opposite direction to Eddie's wandering eye.

We broke up.

Her reply is instant.

It's fate! Hope you got waxed ;)

Of course I did, but Eddie's not going to find out either way. I tut aloud and switch it off. I'm not sure I believe in fate, but I do believe in hard work, grafting and then reaping the fruit of your labour.

'How have you been?' Eddie leans a couple of inches closer to me, ignoring the safety demonstration I'm pretending to be engrossed in. I attempt to steady my rapidly hammering heart, which palpitates rapidly like I'm an animation in a Disney cartoon.

How can he address me is so flippantly, as if I'm no one to him? Though I suppose that's technically what I amounted to, so what else would I expect? And where *is* Maria? I remind myself that I'm not meant to care. I slept with him. He ghosted me. End of story.

Did I mention that it was the best sex of my life? Anyway. That's irrelevant.

'Fine. Thank you.' My eyes remain intently focussed on the stewardess.

'You don't seem to be having a great day.' He runs his thumb thoughtfully over his rugged stubble, amusement flickering in his sideways glancing eyes. If he's referring to my security scene, that was merely the tip of the iceberg.

'You have no idea.' I drag my fingers through my hair and rearrange my dress in an attempt to hide the hint of cleavage, though it has the opposite effect, drawing Eddie's eyes directly there.

His musky aftershave invades the air around me, consuming all rational thought. It's the same scent he wore last September. The memories flood back, washing over me, drowning me with the magnitude of barely squashed emotions. Before I even realise what I'm doing, my fingers take up a life of their own, and the familiar sound of thrumming reverberates from the armrest between us.

'Didn't have you pegged as a Queen fan.' His startling

accuracy and the secret meaning behind his astuteness causes my heart to lurch once again, pumping blood violently through my veins.

'Don't presume to know anything about me,' I growl, though his assertiveness startles me.

He sits quietly for a few minutes, as if he's waiting for me to elaborate on either my day, or my taste in music. It's not going to happen. He's the last person I'm going to confide in.

'I'm sorry,' he says.

I'm unsure if he's apologising that I'm having a shitty day or for his behaviour last September. His tone radiates a certain level of earnestness, but I'd be a fool to trust it. Once bitten, twice shy. Or once shagged, twice dry. Whatever. As I recall, he's the team joker. He'd do anything to raise a giggle. Although right now he looks pretty serious. Emphasis on the pretty, with those enormous oval eyes. It's a good job I'm sworn off men for the next three months. Not that he'd want a repeat anyway. If he did, he wouldn't have disappeared.

His serious pause and throaty swallow lead me to believe the apology refers to Abby's engagement party – or the events that occurred after it, I should say.

'We were drunk.' I acknowledge, not wishing to rehash it.

'I definitely had too much.' He raises an eyebrow and nods with what I can only assume is regret. Does he regret sleeping with me? Huh – not as much as I regret sleeping with him.

'Let's leave it in the past, shall we?' Safer that way.

Even thinking about the way he rejected me causes my stomach to sharply contract. Paul delivered quite enough personal truths for one day. I doubt I can take any more. Not without a kilogram of lemon sherbets to soften the blow. I rustle in my handbag and locate my stash, popping one into my mouth before reluctantly offering him one. Thankfully he declines. At this rate, I'm not sure I have enough to last the day, let alone a week.

The plane moves forward. I grip the armrest near the aisle and close my eyes. We're in the air before I've had the chance to panic. Removing my current romantic read from my handbag, I flip it open pointedly in a feeble attempt to distract myself from the unshakeable memories. He took me so explosively last year, as though it were so much more than just sex. How could he simply disappear? No call. No message. Nothing.

Sneaking a sideward glance at his tanned face, I double-check he's as delicious as my mind regularly conjures him up to be. Wide-set, amorous eyes scorch my skin as he catches me staring. An amused expression indicates he's privy to some 'in joke' that only he gets. Or am I the joke? Is he secretly laughing at me? At how easily he played me?

I return to my book, turning the pages intermittently, but I'm unable to absorb a single word.

'Drinks?' The hostess with the trolley approaches us.

'Yes, please,' Both Eddie and I answer unanimously. I brave meeting his eye.

'White wine, please.' I pull out a twenty-euro note from my bag and pop in another sherbet lemon.

Eddie brushes my hand away and extends a fifty to the lady. 'My shout. Lager, please.'

She places the drinks on our individual fold-down tables and eventually moves on.

'Thank you.' My eyes chance another sideways dart.

'It's the least I can do.' His sheepish smile is orbit shifting. And for a man, he has great skin. It really isn't fair. If things were different I'd pay him to be a poster model for the male skincare range. These rugby players all have sidelines in advertising, what a campaign that would create, though I doubt I could afford him.

I'm unsure if I should return to my book or if that would seem rude after him buying the wine. There's no protocol for this situation. For a woman that can be so decisive, I'm openly rattled. The pages feel heavy as I flip it in my hands.

'Good book?' He squints at the front cover and smirks.

'Fascinating,' I lie.

'Is that why you've read the same page four times?'

'I didn't want to miss anything.' The fevered flush deepens in my cheeks.

'Thank goodness for that. I thought you were just avoiding talking to me.' He lets out a wry chuckle.

'Why on earth would you think that?' I can barely mask the sarcasm from my tone.

'What's it about?' He peers at the front cover again. '*The Seven Year Itch*? What is it, like a porno in a pink cover?' A snigger falls from his lips. He is so blasé. Doesn't he realise the hurt that he caused? Or does he just not care?

'It's slightly pornographic in places,' I admit with a shrug. 'But you know most women need more than just sex in a story. We need mental stimulation.'

'Really? Tell me more, it sounds fascinating.' His sparkling eyes light with mischief. He's toying with me. His witty sense of humour was one of the things I was so attracted to in the first instance.

'The underlying theme is about second chances and making the brave decisions that sometimes go against the grain. The main character married young, for all the wrong reasons, then she meets a man who she really falls in love with, but she's not free to pursue him.'

'That sounds deep. Let me know how it ends.'

'How about I lend it to you when I'm done? You might even learn something.' There goes my big mouth. So much for pretending I don't care. I've never been particularly skilful at hiding my feelings.

'Do you believe everyone deserves a second chance?' That thumb is thoughtfully roaming on his stubble again. I remember it roaming other places. I blink, forcefully blanking it out.

'No.' I take a sip of wine.

'Look, I am truly sorry I didn't call you after that night. I feel like such a shit.' He looks to the table, all trace of a smile gone for once. His fingers pull at the label on his bottle of Budweiser. Wow – two apologies. That's two up on Paul already, not that I'm comparing. Much.

'It's grand,' I lie. It's not grand. Far from it. I agonised over it for weeks, wondering what I'd done to drive him away.

'I'm sure it wasn't your first one-night stand.' I attempt to be mature about it, whilst the little girl lingering inside me silently kicks and screams, *love me, love me, love me*, desperate to have been worth more than just the meeting of a physical need.

'It's complicated, you know?' Eddie glances up at me from under eyelashes that should be illegal on a man.

There's nothing complicated about any of it; he had what he wanted and left, because I stupidly gave it to him on the first night.

'Forget it.' I'm trying my best to. Unsuccessfully, I might add.

'The trouble is I can't.' The hair pricks on my neck. Is he seriously coming on to me now?

'Then maybe you should have called.' It was simple to me.

'It wasn't that easy...' A note of uncertainty in his voice piques my curiosity. Still, I refuse to believe there could be any reason in the world that would justify him not calling me, if he actually wanted to.

'It's irrelevant now.' My teeth grit firmly together. Nothing he can tell me will get him off the hook. The damage is done. I won't be played twice.

He leans back on the headrest, turning towards me in an intimate fashion. A flashback winds me, him looking at me like that once before, from the pillow beside me. My stomach draws up into a tight ball of butterflies that congregate and soar within. With only centimetres between us, the warmth of his breath tickles my lips with each exhale.

'I thought maybe you'd...' he trails off, shaking his head.

I take a large mouthful of chilled wine to break the intensifying eye contact and deliberately change the subject.

'Where is Maria?'

'We fell out.' He shrugs and throws up his hands in a helpless gesture.

'Again?' It's so much easier to talk about them than us.

'She made it very clear yesterday that it's over.' He exhales a weary sigh.

'Why? What did you do?' I hold off on saying 'this time' even though it's on the tip of my tongue. I'm curious why he kept her around for several months, rather than just the one night I was viable for.

'She says I'm emotionally unavailable.' He uses his fingers to make the quotation marks, and a spontaneous burst of laughter tumbles from both of us.

'And are you?' I ask when the laughter subsides. Am I asking for Maria or for myself?

'I thought Abby was the shrink?' Eddie tilts his head at me and presses his full lips together in a smirk. I've said enough.

At least I'm not the only romantic failure. I clink my plastic glass against his half-empty bottle in a silent toast. Though if the newspapers are anything to go by, Eddie and Maria break up and get back together more often than I get my hair blow-dried.

A lopsided smile on his full lips sends a dizzying current racing through my bones. By some mad twist of fate, *The One*

That Got Away is newly single and on his way to the same sunshine resort as me. I almost have to pinch myself. That is until I remember that I never give second chances (unwritten rule 101), and even if I did – I'm sworn off pursuing men at least until the business launch.

CHAPTER FOUR

EDDIE

A wedding abroad was the only way that Callum and Abby could avoid the Irish paparazzi. None of us like to be sneakily photographed six pints into a boozy bender, caught with our trousers (and our dignity) round our ankles, metaphorically speaking, of course. It's unreal the number of journalists that make a living filming, discussing and dissecting celebrity behaviour. We're only fucking human. Everyone needs to let off a bit of steam now and again.

Callum and Abby are waiting for us at the airport, their skin already sun-kissed and glowing, having arrived last week to get organised for their big day. That's one advantage of retirement – Callum is no longer a slave to Coach's strict training schedule and the match list fixtures. I found it practically impossible to get this week off, especially as half the team requested it. Eventually, Coach rearranged training and reluctantly gave us all five days off on the promise that we'd work our butts off on our return.

We have a big match next weekend, against Munster.

Marcus, Ollie, Nathan and I play for Leinster, in addition to playing for our country. It's essential that we win. I reminded Coach when you're training for a marathon, you back off on the mileage in the week leading up to it. Maybe a break is exactly what the team needs. Some of the boys are already here. The rest are flying in over the next two days. The wedding is Wednesday, but Maria insisted we take the full week to make the most of it. I have something to be grateful to her for, at least. I need this break more than I care to admit. And with Emma here, things are more interesting than I could have hoped. The attraction pulls even stronger than it did the first night. It physically tugs at my insides to the point of pain, but pain is my speciality these days. It's something I have had to learn to live with.

The sun splits the stones in the carpark. The powder blue sky is without a single cloud. The pilot announced that the outside temperature was twenty-six degrees. I'm feeling the heat, and it's not just the weather.

Abby throws her arms around Emma. 'So, you guys found each other?' She's about as subtle as a ten-tonne lorry reversing in, with luminous hazard lights flashing. She'd been the same way last year, insisting I go out with her friend, declaring we were a match made in heaven. She wasn't wrong, though it turned out that the timing, unfortunately, was.

Callum extends a firm hand to shake mine, his sleeping baby daughter cradled in his other arm. She's an absolute beauty. He's lucky to have two women to call his own.

'Where's Paul?' Abby asks Emma.

Who is Paul? It didn't occur to me that Emma might have a boyfriend. She didn't mention it on the three-hour flight. Mind you, why would she tell me anything after the way I treated her? Although the way I caught her widening eyes roaming over me, I dared to think for a second that maybe she might consider giving me a second chance, like that damn book she was pretending to be intrigued in.

Callum takes Emma's luggage before I can, and begins telling me how great the resort is, drowning out her answer regarding the infamous Paul, which I'm now dying to hear.

We pile into Callum's rental jeep, a Range Rover no less. There's nothing small about Callum Connolly. The girls hop into the back, cooing over the baby. I sit up front, trying to eavesdrop.

If Emma's boyfriend is coming to the wedding, wouldn't they have arrived together? When she mellowed towards me on the flight, for a split second, I'd dared to wonder if maybe we could pick up where we left off. Now I know she's not outwardly horrified by what I'd done. She would be, though, if she knew what had happened, the demon rears its ugly head and bitterly reminds me.

'How's Matthew?' Callum enquires politely after my brother.

'He's okay. Getting on with it. Actually, I put an offer on a place for him today. It's five doors down from mine. I'm hoping it might make the transition easier on him, you know?'

Callum nods and pats my shoulder. 'It was such a dreadful shame, what happened.'

I can't go over it now, and certainly not in front of Emma. It's too raw. I deliberately change the subject. 'Abby, how are you feeling about marrying Ireland's most eligible bachelor, Callum *Touch Down* Connolly?' I give him a dig in the leg to show I'm joking.

'The only thing he's touching down now is me.' Abby squeals at her own joke. Callum had a huge reputation with the ladies before he hooked up with Ireland's favourite agony aunt. Mind you, my own reputation isn't far behind. Though, unlike Callum, I've never been averse to settling down. It's just I never met the right one. Or if I did, I didn't realise it. Maybe Maria is right? Maybe I am 'emotionally unavailable', whatever that even means.

I have an inability to be serious; it's just my way of dealing with things. Though I've had to work harder lately to uphold my reputation as the team joker, disguising the recent horror that lurks behind the laughter.

The journey from the airport to the resort takes thirty minutes. Callum brings us along the coastline. The sparkling sea boasts an unnerving clarity as it swells against the shore, contrasted by a darker, vivid velvety blue further out. Rolling hills with scattered villages dot the landscape. The scenery is out of this world, photos fail to capture its raw beauty. We frequently travel as a team, but I've seen nothing that compares to this.

I glance round to see Emma hanging on to the interior of the door, her fingernails practically pierce the leather as she glances warily at the flimsy metal barrier that separates the road from a hundred metre drop off the cliffside into the Adriatic Sea. It seems the beauty business queen is afraid of heights as well as flying, from the way she gripped the arm rest on the plane. She has a reputation for being a ball-breaker, but so far today, I've seen several of her fears, even the one she tries to hide the most- the fear of me sucking her in and spitting her out again. I won't do it to her, instead I'll put my own selfish physical desires aside and show her the respect that she deserves. And what she deserves, is so much more than I can offer her.

Arriving at the hotel, I realise I'm looking at Callum's wet dream. The Oceania is ultra-modern, sleek and chic, predominantly compromised of glass and granite. Enormous white pillars frame the doorway, and a red carpet extends into the carpark, where a commotion seems to be occurring. Callum tuts at a woman in her fifties rowing stridently with a man wearing a suit that has to be sweltering in this heat.

'Oh no!' Abby groans. 'That's my mother arguing with the manager. What's wrong with her now?'

Callum chuckles and gives me a knowing look; buckle up, the show is about to begin. He lowers the window to listen, but remains in his seat, hiding safely away from the dispute with Emma and me. Abby leaps out the second the engine cuts out.

'Mam, what is it? What now?' Abby sounds exasperated. I get the impression this isn't the first drama that Mrs Queenan has instigated this week.

'It's Paolo here. He tells me he has no suite available for the Murphys. I'm after telling him they have travelled *all the way* from the east coast of Ireland to be here for *my* daughter's wedding, and he has no room for them!'

'That's because *we* didn't invite them,' Callum mutters to me. '*She* did.'

'We have a sister hotel with availability. It's only fifteen minutes away. I will arrange a private transfer.' Paolo appears to be doing his best to rectify the situation. Sweat beads on his forehead, and a glint of panic flickers in his crinkling eyes.

'They don't want a private transfer. They want a suite here. It's preposterous.' Mrs Queenan wails, her arms flying excessively in the air.

A smartly dressed receptionist arrives with a clipboard and a pen. 'We have a room that's being vacated tomorrow. And we nearly always have a no show. We will do our best to accommodate everyone here,' she assures an increasingly difficult Mrs Queenan.

'I should think so, and could we not do this in the reception area? Why are we out here sweating like pilgrims?' Apparently, there is no appeasing Abby's mother today.

'We are out here, Madam, because you insisted that I

personally carry your friend's luggage in from the car park,' Paolo reminds her.

Callum winces next to me. 'Always some family fucking drama with my new mother-in-law.'

'If it's any help with numbers, Maria isn't coming. We broke up — in case you somehow missed the media shitstorm she invoked yesterday. If there's a single room or something, I'm happy to take it,' I tell Callum to be helpful.

'You guys always break up.' Callum dismisses my revelation as if it means nothing.

'This time it's for real.' For once, my features don't flicker. I'm deadly serious.

'Seriously?' Callum cocks his head to one side attentively.

'Finito. Thank god.' The relief in my tone reassures Callum enough to express his true feelings on the matter.

'She's no good for you, man. I don't like telling you your business, but she's too high maintenance. And that business at Wimbledon, you know there's no smoke without fire.'

'I'm beginning to see that.' I clear my throat noisily, not wishing to discuss it any further.

Emma stares at us, opening her mouth to say something, but closes it abruptly again. Callum turns his head and squints at her. 'You okay?'

'Paul's not coming either. That's another space free.' She looks at the floor, anywhere but at me. I'm yet to confirm whether he's her boyfriend or not, and I'm battling to remember that it's not supposed to matter.

Callum taps the steering wheel thoughtfully for a few seconds.

'Guys, I absolutely hate to put this on you, but is there any chance you'd consider bunking in together for a night? Looks like there will be more space tomorrow, and they're not just bedrooms. They're more like one-bedroom apartments. I'd give up mine, but Abby has it crammed with wedding stuff, and we need the space for the baby. We could give the Murphys yours, Eddie? What do you think?'

I glance at Emma, who stares pointedly out of the window, anywhere but at me. White knuckles clench and flex. She exhales a heavy sigh and rolls her eyes skywards, before shrugging noncommittally at me.

'I suppose I could put up with him, *if* it's only one night.'

Huh! She managed to put up with me for a night once before! If I remember rightly, she even seemed to enjoy it. If I'd thought she'd mellowed towards me on the flight, I was clearly mistaken. Still, it's probably safer this way.

'There will be plenty of space, I promise. Please, guys, Cathy Queenan's about to burst a blood vessel,' Callum pleads.

'It's fine with me.' I battle with the upward curling of a smile. It's more than fucking fine. It's like Christmas. Me, stuck sharing a bedroom with the sexiest woman I've ever been acquainted with. If I was anyway decent, I'd stay away from her, for her own sake. But now, the decision has been taken out of my hands, and my own selfish desires are running wild once again at this little twist of fate.

It's kind of mad that the two of us are here, me newly single, her potentially single. It reminds me of a bad rom-com starring that plonker Matthew McConaughey. Things are looking up. There was something explosive between us last year. Maybe, just maybe, I will be able to remind her of it.

CHAPTER FIVE

EMMA

The receptionist takes my reservation details while Eddie lurks behind silently.

'You are in one of our honeymoon suites. The views are outstanding, and there is a jacuzzi bath big enough for two.' The receptionist smiles and nods at us.

'What? That isn't what I booked. Abby and Callum are the ones getting married... There must be some kind of mistake.' The blush rises up my neck, creeping into my cheeks.

She frowns at her computer screen momentarily, then smiles again.

'We have several honeymoon suites. Many VIPs come to this hotel. You are Emma Harvey?'

'I am.'

'Then you booked this suite.' Her clipped voice projects an unquestionable certainty.

Now I think of it, I'd booked it after a few glasses of wine one Friday night. In fact, I vaguely remember having a daft idea that all the romance might inspire Paul to get down on one knee. Oh my god, he was right! I was so desperate for that ring, even if it meant marrying the wrong man! How could I get it so wrong? Shame envelops me, but I push it away and remind myself this is precisely why I decided to focus purely on the new business.

As I sign the paperwork, she issues two keycards before pointing us toward the lifts. The reception area boasts a triple-height glass ceiling, and the floor appears to be solid white marble. Every corner of the place screams wealth and luxury. Scanning the room, I attempt to memorise every detail. If I could even mirror a hint of this style in the new premises, it will ooze magnificence.

'Meet us in the bar in an hour?' Abby calls to my retreating back, distracted with the arrival of more of her guests. I hope these ones are actually invited.

'Sure.' I look at my watch; it's almost seven. We lost an hour with the time difference.

'You too, Eddie. Everyone will be there.' Abby waves and offers a flick of her wrist, motioning us to hurry. I don't miss the sly wink and mischievous pearly grin she delivers. Neither does Eddie.

Funny that the day I decide I'm taking a break from men, I'm forced to share a room with the one I wasted Christmas pining over. I would possibly have killed for this opportunity a year ago. Not now. Today it's merely an inconvenience.

His rejection hurt. Primarily because, as cheesy as it sounds, I really felt we'd had a deep, earth-moving connection. I hate the term *connection*. Usually, the person using it is twenty years my senior, six stone heavier, or neglects to mention he's already married.

Eddie found a connection alright, but it was merely a physical one.

In the lift, he takes the room key and presses the button.

I look anywhere but at him. The scent of his aftershave surrounds me, tinged with a more masculine smell, one that I can only assume is a product of this heat. As much as I want to fight the attraction, he still draws me in, magnetically manhandling my emotions.

Peeking at his broad frame standing confidently in front of me, I groan internally. His hair falls lazily over one eye, sweeping across insanely high cheekbones. This man needs no help with contouring. He is ripped in all the right places. I exhale slowly. Thank god it's only one night.

The lift doors silently slide open, and Eddie carries both of our bags down the corridor, biceps bulging in that indecently tight white T-shirt. Huh, no point pretending he's a gentleman now. He's months too late. He's probably on the rebound now, looking for a way to give Maria the two fingers before publicly and passionately making up with her. There's no way I'm getting in the middle of that shitshow.

We reach room 425, my room, our room. Whatever. Eddie opens the door. The last rays of light burst in the floor-to-ceiling windows from the rapidly descending sun as it drops spectacularly from the topaz sky. A golden fire-like glow cascades across brilliant white furniture, extending all the way to a lavish queen-sized bed at the far side of the enormous room. It's as if it's lighting the pathway directly to the rose petal covered sheets. It couldn't possibly be any more romantic.

The huge jacuzzi bath that the receptionist had mentioned sits in the centre of the bedroom, large enough to comfortably fit eight people, never mind two. A bottle of champagne sits in an ice bucket next to it, alongside two crystal flutes.

'Wow. Paul was really planning on pulling out all the stops for you. Shame he couldn't make it.' Eddies whistles lowly and bites his lip.

Huh! Paul was planning nothing of the sort. I organised this all by my delusional self. Ignoring his remarks, I head straight out to the balcony to watch the sun set over the Adriatic Sea and to put some distance between us. Annoyingly, Eddie follows me out. The stainless-steel balcony railing is covered in a bright decorative floral foliage. I check it's sturdy with one hand before daring to put my weight on it.

'It's out of this world.' Eddie exhales the words dreamily, more to himself than me.

It takes less than four minutes for the sun to sink spectacularly. We stand side by side, immersed in our own thoughts.

'I'll take the couch, obviously.' Eddie breaks the silence, turning to head back inside, I assume to unpack.

With the wine wearing off and the knowledge that we are stuck sharing the honeymoon suite, the awkwardness creeps back in. I follow him inside in pursuit of a hot shower. Walking through the luxurious accommodation for a closer inspection, I register with a sense of horror that the suite has no doors.

The sofa and coffee table are positioned fifteen foot from the bed, but they are still in the same room. I glance around for a bathroom. There's an archway to the right of the bed. My teeth clench as I approach. Even the bathroom doesn't have a door! He'll be able to hear me pee, watch me shower! Blood pools in my cheeks as I realise it will work both ways. If I felt awkward before, this is on a whole new skin-crawling cringe chart.

While Eddie rummages in his holdall, I address the problem directly, despite my underlying embarrassment. 'I see this place doesn't care much for privacy. I hope you don't snore. I'll sit on the balcony while you shower. You can head to the bar while I get ready.' My room, my rules.

Eddie sniggers. Life is one big joke to him. Everything is one big game, especially women. And this is not an even playing field because he has one distinct advantage; I know he's the perfect score.

'Or we could just hop in the bath together. It would save a bit of time if we didn't have to wait to take turns...' A devilish smirk strains his lips into an upwards curl.

'No chance. And if you carry on like that, you'll be looking for a new roomie.'

Sauntering outside again, I stare at the twilight, inhaling the scent of freshly cut grass and sun cream. He emerges twenty minutes later, wearing khaki shorts and a black polo shirt, almost the same shade as his floppy hair.

'Sure you don't want me to wait for you?'

'I think I can find my own way to the bar.'

'I'll have a glass of white wine waiting for you. It seems to make you a little less hostile towards me.' Eddie winks, grazes my cheek with a warm invasive brush of his lips, and issues a small smile as he departs.

Who does he think he is?

And hostile? Me? I wasn't the one that never called! Okay, I am bearing a grudge, despite my best efforts. I need to rein it in.

CHAPTER SIX

EDDIE

I decide to familiarise myself with the resort before heading to the bar and am instinctively drawn to the almost empty beach. The nearly full moon casts a luminous glow on a couple in the distance, racing towards the sea practically naked. The laughter that erupts from them is infectious, and I catch myself laughing along with them, a ripple of envy washing over me. The man flicks water at the woman, and she shrieks with laughter. It's only as I get closer that I realise it's Callum and Abby. Anyone can see that they are completely enamoured with each other. A creeping sensation of envy curls at my insides.

Being around Emma is harder than I anticipated, and not just because I'm unbelievably attracted to her. I told myself I wouldn't flirt with her, but as soon as I open my mouth, the lines just roll off my tongue. I can't help myself. Being with her reminds me of that night, the night before my life was transformed beyond recognition. Emma reminds me of who I was before then; carefree and more than a little immature. Unfortunately, I've had to grow up a bit since then.

Out of habit, I pull my phone from my pocket and check the screen. A text from my sister Keira illuminates the screen.

Outbid on Matthew's house. How far are you willing to go?

I was half prepared for this, so my reply is instant and automatic. Fixing some of the wrong I've committed is the only way I might be able to fix myself.

Whatever it takes.

Trudging up the beach with my hands tucked into my pockets, I reach the bar. Low lighting and soft acoustic music create a relaxed atmosphere. My teammates, Marcus, Ollie, and Nathan, wave me over from the table that they're congregated around.

Marcus is the team captain, a brute of a man. Underneath his ridiculously hairy chest, his ribcage encases a heart of solid gold. Ollie is our flanker, recently separated from his long-term girlfriend, and Nathan is the team's baby. At only twenty-four years old, he has already managed to father a child with his childhood sweetheart. Unfortunately things didn't stay too sweet for long after that. After a difficult legal battle, Nathan eventually managed to settle out of court and now has access to his little girl three days each week.

Callum's brother Brian waves across the room from a table where he sits with his wife, his father, and his aunt. We're all well acquainted with each other's family at this stage, meeting regularly at matches and for drinks in the player's lounge afterwards.

'Look what the cat dragged in! I heard you are shacked up with Abby's friend already. Fast-mover Harrington! You've been single for what...twenty-four hours?' Marcus bellows, wiggling his eyebrows suggestively.

I fist pump each of them in greeting, trying to hide the smirk that's threatening to take over my entire face. Much as I shouldn't be, I can't deny the fact that I am happy about the recent twist of fate that sees me sharing with Emma.

'So, are you guys going to rekindle that spark or what?' Nathan leans forward, resting an elbow on the table. 'Because if not...I wouldn't mind hammering that one over the line. Have you seen the body on her? I cannot wait to get to the pool in the morning for a better look.'

Lewd comments in the changing rooms are ten a penny, but my smirk transforms into a full-blown frown at Nathan's blatant disrespect for Emma.

'She's off-limits,' I warn him, pulling up a chair next to him.

'Alright, Harrington, no need to get lairy. I was only joking. I got my eye on the little one over there.' He takes a sip of his drink and points out one of Abby's friends that we met at the engagement party. Kelly? No, Kerry, I think her name is. She can't be more than five foot four, but she's cute for sure.

Callum enters the bar from the poolside doors, with Abby hanging off his arm, both of them bright-eyed and red-cheeked, carrying their shoes in their hands.

'It's your round.' Marcus gives me the excuse I need to escape the banter and think for a second.

Leaning against the bar, I wait to be served and for the angry hammering to resolve in my heart. Nathan is perfectly entitled to go after Emma, Kerry or any other woman he wants. So why does the thought of it being Emma make me physically fume? Until today, I hadn't laid eyes on her in almost a year. I have absolutely no claim on her. I've only just untangled myself from the mess with Maria. Am I seriously going to start something new already? Though it isn't entirely new, more like an old flame that's burning brighter than ever. Despite her earlier comment and my earlier intentions to leave her be, I clearly haven't entirely ruled out the possibility of a second chance.

I've been flirting with Emma since the second I met her. Even back then, I knew she was something special. I wanted her then, and I still want her. But what I want and what I deserve are two entirely different things. Though if I'm truthful with myself that won't stop me from pursuing her. Her blatant refusal to entertain the idea only drives me to try harder. Now I've seen her again, the memories have been unleashed, and with the threat of someone else staking a claim, I realise I have to have her again.

Instinctively, I glance to the door as she enters the bar. She looks sensational in a pair of tight white jeans and gold stilettos, and my heart rate quickens again. It's not even a want... It's a deep-rooted need.

I order a round of drinks, including Emma's afore promised wine, and embark on a plan to prove that I can be so much more than the man who never called.

CHAPTER SEVEN

EMMA

Karen and Kerry sit at a round table with Karen's girlfriend Fran, and a jug containing an exotic looking turquoise concoction between them. They flew in yesterday, and from the way they're lounging around the bar, they have settled in exceptionally well already.

Kerry wears a white jumpsuit, probably purchased in the kids' department of Debenhams. She's so petite she's like a china doll. Standing with a wobble, she throws her arms around me. Her grey glassy eyes glint a little too brightly. It looks like I have some catching up to do.

'Emma! You made it.'

'Not without a few complications. How are you all?' I kiss each one of them on the cheek, delighted to fall into their familiar banter. Kerry, Karen and I have been friends since school. We have a lot of shared history, from first kisses to first jobs and everything in between.

'Where's Paul?' Fran looks behind me.

'Working. And no longer my problem, by the way. But don't worry, I've acquired a new one since then. You know I have a knack for attracting them.' I motion for the barman to bring us another pitcher and fresh glasses. I think we're going to need it.

'Anything to do with Hooker Harrington at the bar over there?' Karen's eyebrows lift beneath her fringe. Her blue-black bob sports one of her quirky trademark headbands; this one is scarlet with an enormous side bow.

'You mean my new roommate?'

'You are fucking joking me! Ten to one says you shag him tonight.' Kerry is officially as drunk as I suspected.

'Hah! Thanks a million, girls. Been there, done that. You know I don't give second chances. Besides, I'm taking a break from the romantic rat race, going to channel all my energy into the new spa. There's a lot to be done in the next three months.' Even as the words fall from my mouth, my insides quiver at the sight of him.

'Can't you take a break when we get home? A little holiday fling might be just what the doctor ordered.' Kerry licks her lips in a deliberately suggestive fashion and giggles.

That exact thought had crossed my mind, but no, I won't give in to him, not even for a meaningless holiday no-strings-attached fling, assuming he seriously wants me to. I can't afford to be broken-hearted and pining over him *again,* not when I'm about to take the biggest career plunge of my life. So much still has to be done; securing the new property, final-ising the product design, launching the marketing campaign. I'm still waiting for the final round of product testing to be approved. The last thing I need is a distraction.

'What about the tennis player, Maria?' Karen asks.

'Gone. By all accounts, it's over.' I shrug.

'You're doing that weird finger tapping again.' Kerry puts

her hand over mine to stop the table rattling beneath the subconscious blows from my long fingers.

Shit, she's right. No matter how much I tell myself I'm off men, not to even consider him as an option, my subconscious continues to torture me with hardcore multi-coloured memories of that night. His body writhing on top of mine, grinding, pushing, thrusting. It was an eventful night. I thought hat tricks were only for footballers.

The chemistry is undeniably explosive. Would it be possible to just have sex, get it out of our systems and go our separate ways? Doubtful. It would break all my rules, and my heart when he inevitably crawled back to Maria.

I sit back, letting the fruity cocktail slip down the back of my throat slowly, while Karen reinforces all the reasons I should religiously abide by dating rule 101 and erase all thoughts of a fling with Eddie from my mind.

'He lied to you, used you and then disappeared into the sunset without so much as a backwards glance.'

It's only the truth, but it still hurts.

Abby approaches from across the bar and signals Callum to push a table against ours. She catches the tail end of the conversation.

'Eddie's not a bad guy, Em. I wouldn't have tried to set you up in the first place if he was.' Abby adopts her radio presenter voice, the one which I assume she thinks is the most convincing.

'Why does everyone think I care?' I swallow another mouthful of sugary blue liquid.

'He likes you, Emma.' Callum nods knowingly as he shoves the neighbouring table against ours and gestures to his teammates to join us. Fucking fantastic.

'There's a lot more to Eddie than you know.'

Abby looks as blank as the rest of us, apparently also in

the dark about Eddie's secret depth. A niggle of curiosity stirs within, but there's no time to ask any more questions as three of Callum's former teammates, Marcus, Ollie, and Nathan migrate across the room towards us, clutching their pint glasses. They pull out chairs at the table next to us and call Eddie over from the bar.

'Hoping for some Sex On The Beach, Emma?' Marcus asks with a crude grin that exposes a big gap between his two front teeth. He is notoriously loud-mouthed, but Abby swears he's like a giant cuddly teddy bear underneath the bolshy exterior.

Eddie approaches with a tray full of drinks. His jawline is tight in a grimace at Marcus's remarks. 'Marcus won't be happy until he has every single one of his mates married off. He's like a mother hen. He's even growing a pair of feckin' tits to feed us with.' Eddie tweaks Marcus's nipple through his shirt and digs him in the ribs. Marcus responds by pulling him into a headlock.

I deliberately avoid looking at Eddie, but he manages to sneak his way into the seat directly across from me. Pushing over a bottle of white wine, he winks at me meaningfully. I fight the urge to laugh, to give him the satisfaction of making me do so. He's not allowed to joke with me. My heart can't take his games.

One round rolls into another. Then another. Most of the conversation is centred around the resort, the upcoming wedding and the plans for the next few days. A foot brushes gently against my ankle underneath the table. The first time I dismiss it as an accident. The second time, I raise my eyes enough to meet Eddie's mischievously glinting eyes.

What is he playing at? I'm unsure whether to be flattered that he's still feeling the attraction or insulted that he thinks he can just pick me up from where he left me, one year on.

The alcohol begins to take its toll. My empty stomach

churns as I've eaten almost nothing the entire day. It seems I'm not the only one; Kerry's eyes roll theatrically into her head.

'Guys, I'm going to head up to bed. I'm shattered. I'll see you for breakfast, yeah?'

'Are you okay?' Karen whispers, standing with me. She places her arms loosely around my shoulders. We've been friends since we were twelve. There's not a lot I can hide from her, although she tried to hide a lot from us for years. Namely her sexuality. Not that any of us care who she loves, as long as they are good to her. And thankfully, Fran is good to her.

'I don't know,' I tell her truthfully.

I'm a bit lost, newly single and more than a bit shaken by Eddie's proximity. It's all very well deciding to focus on a business, but it's easier said than done when I'm in a romantic resort with a steaming hot rugby player who seems to want a replay of one of the best nights of my life.

Karen squeezes my arm supportively. She offers a conspiring wink as she steps back to let me pass. 'I'll head up with you. I'm going to see Kerry to her room. On "The Kerry-O'Metre" she's about a nine.' The Kerry-O'Meter started when we were eighteen and clubbing four nights of the week. She never could handle her drink. She's not a bad drunk by any means, but she's likely to fall asleep or spontaneously projectile vomit if she reaches a ten.

'Want Nathan to walk you to your room, Emma?' Marcus offers. Perhaps he hasn't heard I've already agreed to share my room with another one of his teammates tonight? Or maybe he's trying to stir the pot? Nathan's fit alright, if you like that shaggy blond surfer look. Unfortunately for me, I'm more into the tall, dark, and apparently emotionally unavailable type.

'I'll see you later...' Eddie says meaningfully.

'Ah ha. I see where this is going! You two *are* going to pick up where you left off,' Marcus bellows.

'No chance,' I say, at the same time as Eddie says, 'Here's hoping.'

CHAPTER EIGHT

EMMA

In the bathroom, I wonder for a second if I should sleep with concealer on, before shaking my head at my own ridiculous vanity. Perhaps if he sees me at my worst, he won't be tempted to crack on to me again, and I won't be tempted to say yes.

Opening my case, I realise that I didn't pack any pyjamas. I don't normally wear them and didn't anticipate company – well, other than Paul. Oh god, the last thing I want to do now is lie awake beating myself up about Paul's parting remarks. He was right about everything. It slapped me in the face like a wet fish when I saw this place; the honeymoon suite and the champagne. Thank god he wasn't here to witness it. I was so desperate to bag myself a husband that I would have undoubtedly accepted a proposal from a man I knew deep down, wasn't right for me.

Why am I so desperate to find a husband? Simply to satisfy my mother? Or is it more than that? Seeing Abby settling with Callum certainly magnified my lifelong quest. I dream of what they have. Not the celebrity lifestyle, or the fancy cars and VIP parties, but the depth of their love, that sense of finding the other part of yourself, because truth be told, I've always felt a part of me is missing.

I scan the room for something to throw on. My scrutinising gaze falls onto Eddie's open holdall. A short-sleeved Ireland rugby jersey pokes out from the top. I grab it and pull it over my head without overthinking it. It smells of his unique scent; a substantial squirt of aftershave, and a hint of masculine sweat, tinged with a lavender laundry powder.

Scraping the wasted, withering rose petals from the bed, I pull back the Egyptian cotton and fall into the comfort of the cool crisp sheets. For a woman that usually struggles to fall asleep, tonight, my heavy eyelids close. Emotionally, I'm exhausted.

A loud thud followed by a low 'fuck' awakens me from a curiously disturbing dream in which I was wandering the beach, barefoot and alone, searching for somebody. The anguish was so real that a dewy perspiration lines my forehead, and the twisted knots in my stomach remain, even as my eyes open. I don't know who I was supposed to be searching for, but my desperation to find them was tangible. Bolting upright rapidly, I bunch the covers around myself protectively.

'Eddie?' There's an audible anguish in my whisper; a distinct sense of vulnerability overwhelms me. I'm a woman, alone in a foreign country. Okay, my friends are all in the same hotel, but what good are they to me if some maniac breaks into my room?

Fumbling around in the dark, I manage to flick on the bedside lamp, partially shielding my eyes from the intrusive brightness with my hands. Eddie stands at the bottom of the bed, squinting, that lopsided smile revealing a flash of perfect porcelain. The top two buttons of his shirt are undone, and his hands are tucked casually in his short pockets. Examining him, I digest the curves of his contours as an earthquake trembles within me. How can someone who plays contact sport for a living be so handsome?

'Is that my shirt you're wearing?' His open admiration turns my insides from twisted knots to instant mush.

'Sorry.' A blush creeps up my cheeks at being caught. 'I didn't pack any pyjamas.' I trail off, realising I'm only incriminating myself further.

'It looks great on you.' He folds his arms over his chest and continues to gaze at me, eyes blackening with a building intensity.

'I only meant to borrow it. I'll give it back to you.' My mouth is dry. The words come out jilted, stammered. If I was concerned he'd notice the pigmentation on my naked face, I needn't worry. His eyes are firmly trained on my body.

'What if I said I want it back now?' He continues to play mercilessly with me.

I lick my lips and swallow hard. I've had more X-rated dreams about this man than I'd admit to any person alive, and now here he is, standing over my bed, practically daring me to give in to him. Dark pupils burn into mine, but even if I hadn't just sworn off men, he is number one on my long list of unsuitable suitors.

Ignoring his suggestive question, I pluck an imaginary feather from the duvet and brush it to the floor. 'The sofa is just behind you.'

Could it really be over between him and Maria this time? And if it is, what might that possibly mean for us? My heart won't survive it if he uses me again, but my body might not survive it if he doesn't. Knowing he's here, in the same room as me, is almost too much. I switch the lamp off and cover my face with a pillow to silence my scream of mind-boggling frustration.

CHAPTER NINE

EDDIE

The rapidly rising sun infiltrates the cracks of the heavy velvet curtains, and for a second, I wonder where I am. My back is in bits after spending the night on the couch. I lift my head to peek at Emma, but all I can see is a mass of chestnut hair fanning over the plump pillows and one deliciously long leg poking out from under the covers, indecently gathering the duvet in a place that I can only dream of.

The chemistry is unquestionably still there. Does Emma think she can hide it from me? Or is Paul still occupying the space in her heart? The thought of her with another man sends a searing stabbing jealousy through my insides. Though I have no right to feel that way after the way I left things the last time, especially when I stupidly fell into bed with Maria Vaillancourt. She was only ever a distraction, nothing more.

I can't undo any of it, with Emma or anyone else, but the last few months have taught me exactly what I don't want in my life. In contrast, it's becoming clear that Emma is what I *do* want.

I pull on a pair of shorts, a training vest and a pair of runners and creep quietly out of the room in search of the gym. I'm a morning person, always have been, probably always will be. I'm addicted to exercise, to the rush of adrenaline that surges through every single cell as I push my body to its absolute maximum, testing the limits of my own strength. Whenever my demons threaten to take over, clouding my mind, I hit the weights or the treadmill, preferably both.

The hotel gym is spacious and boasts a phenomenal amount of machinery. I sign in, grab a towel and bottle of water and hit the treadmill. The only other person in there is Callum.

'Dude, you're supposed to be on holiday,' I tell him. His days of worrying about maintaining his fitness are gone. Now he's in the commentating box in a crisp fitting suit, under the spotlight of a very different camera to us.

'Yeah, but didn't you hear? The television adds ten pounds,' he says with a chuckle. He has no concerns there. From the look of things on the beach last night, Abby seems to burn a whole heap of his energy.

'How did it go with Emma last night?' Callum turns to look at me without pausing his machine. He's just showing off. Any normal person would fall flat on their face – especially one who had major heart surgery only a year earlier. I up the speed on my own machine and look only at the mirrored wall in front of us.

'When I got up there, she was in bed already.'

'And?' Callum hits the emergency stop button on his treadmill and stares at me panting before taking a swig of his water.

'And nothing. Unless you count her wearing my shirt as a nightdress, which by the way she looked fucking incredible in.' My feet pound harder as I hammer out all of my sexual frustration.

'She wouldn't wear your shirt if she hates you.' Callum smirks.

'I wouldn't count on it. Though there is definitely some sort of energy burning there. What about Paul?'

'It's over, according to Abby. I told you last year, and I'm telling you again. You two are made for each other. You just don't know it yet.'

'Huh. The only time Emma spoke to me willingly was on the flight, and that was because she had a huge glass of wine in her hand, and we were stuck in a confined space.' Emma has me pegged as the team joker, but she has no idea. The truth is, I'm just a joke. I fuck up everything that I touch.

Callum wipes the beading sweat on his forehead with a towel and slaps me on the back. 'Well, I've provided you the confined space. All you have to do is pour the wine.' He saunters out of the gym with a parting wink.

Easy for him to say, with his gorgeous fiancée and bouncing baby girl, but at least now I know Emma is actually single. It makes the path to winning her over clearer. Wait, is that what I'm seriously going to attempt? I haven't even been single for forty-eight hours. But when I think about it, *if* I'm going to pursue her, it has to be for something more than another meaningless fling, otherwise, I am exactly the selfish twat she thinks I am. I hurt her once. I can't do it again.

All my adult life, I've struggled to find a meaningful relationship, though I probably haven't helped myself with my endless clowning around. There's been no real challenge; women have come easily, mind you, they've gone just as easily too. There's only so much messing around a man can do before it becomes boring.

The truth is I *am* ready to settle. I've been ready to find the right person for some time. Last year, at Callum's engagement, I really thought I'd found that person in Emma, but then circumstances prevented me from pursuing it.

I long for what Callum has – a solid woman by my side and a family while I'm young enough to enjoy them. Family is everything to me. I count my siblings among my closest friends. Most weeks, we congregate at either Mam and Dad's, or Keira's, for the traditional roast. The grown-ups drink wine and the kids run riot. I usually run after them, the big child that I am, and while I'm busy chasing kids, I can successfully avoid the adult scrutiny.

They urged me repeatedly to bring Maria to dinner, but I couldn't. Firstly, I knew she would hate it. She hates kids, noise and chaos, and that's exactly what Harrington family dinners involve. And secondly, I knew deep down that I had no intention of creating something lasting with her.

I turn up the tempo again, blood pounds through my limbs and my heart hammers in my ears. I'm almost at my maximum speed, now to see how long I can hang on like this for. It's a fine line between pleasure and pain. The adrenaline spikes and the rush of endorphins crusade through me. The rush is addictive, the high empowering, offering a false sense of invincibility, in this very rush, I feel I could take over the world.

Callum's parting words echo through my mind. Emma is single. I'm single. Despite her repeated knock backs, maybe the stars are finally aligning for us? There's an unfinished, burning energy when it comes to us, and instead of fizzling out in the year that we've been apart, it appears to have multiplied.

That night with her was one of the best of my life. If I could get her to lower her carefully constructed guard, maybe, just maybe, I could convince her to engage in a replay? A do-over? A second chance, as undeserving as I may be.

Using a hotel issued hand towel, I wipe the sweat from my face and head back to the room with an endorphin-charged positivity. I push open the door slowly, quietly, in case she's still asleep. She isn't, but she's still in bed, wearing my shirt.

'Good morning.' I head straight to the fancy coffee machine, press the on button and sift through a multitude of coloured capsules while it heats up.

'Hi.' She smiles at me, but there's a wariness in her tone. Unsurprising, I suppose, given our history. Her fingers drag her hair over her face, almost as if she's trying to hide from me.

'Emma, I was thinking...maybe we could just—'

'No, Eddie. We can't do anything. Stop looking at me like that. It's not going to happen. I'm going for a shower.' She pulls a hairband over her forehead and struts towards her case, to rummage through her belongings. I stare at her long, tanned legs, a low whistle escapes me.

'No peeking,' she warns, still not fully facing me. Why is she trying to hide from me? She's fucking beautiful. Maybe she just can't bear to look at me after everything? Shit, I feel that way myself most days. I persevere anyway.

'I've seen it all before,' I remind her, but she refuses to look up.

'You won't be seeing it again.' She flicks her hair off her face aggressively, almost as though she's challenging me, but to do what, I don't know.

Clusters of tiny freckles adorn her cheekbones, bestowing an innocence usually associated with adolescence. She looks less fierce without her usual make-up. She's naturally beautiful, but there's an air of vulnerability about her that I've never noticed before.

'I can be very persuasive when I want something. Not to mention persistent.'

'And what is it exactly that you want, Eddie? Because, as I

recall, you already had it.' Her legs are hip-width apart, her hand positioned firmly on the curve of her hip.

'I want another chance. And I'm willing to work for it.'

'Not going to happen. Been there, done that, got the T-shirt.' She gestured to the one she's wearing. Her mouth says one thing, but her eyes continue to flick over my body.

'I'll play dirty if I have to.'

'You'll be playing with yourself.' Her swaying backside disappears into the bathroom. I decide to pull out the big guns. Literally. I take off my damp gym shirt and shorts and deliberately wait in my boxers for my turn in the shower, hoping my morning glory goes down enough not to poke her eye out on the way past.

Eventually, Emma emerges from the bathroom in a white dress which can only be described as fit for the beach. It's practically see-through for a start; the white bikini underneath is as clear as if she had nothing on over it. I battle not to stare, momentarily forgetting that I'm not wearing a lot myself.

She looks up, her bare feet skidding to an abrupt standstill. Her eyes roam over my bare chest, as I'd intended. As I pass by her, I brush unnecessarily close to her, close enough for my front to graze her side. A quick glance at the reflection in the bathroom mirror captures her in the exact same spot, a rabbit in the headlights. I turn the shower back on.

'That's not fair, Eddie Harrington!'

With my back to her, I drop my boxers, giving her a full view of my toned backside, before stepping into the swirling steam of the shower.

I can't contain the laughter that erupts from my chest. It catches in my throat as I realise there's nothing funny about having a raging boner in the shower and having the woman I'm dying to share it with laughing from ten feet away.

CHAPTER TEN

EMMA

Breakfast is served in the main dining hall, overlooking the gentle lulling waves of the glittering turquoise sea. The waitress takes my room number and leads me to a small table for one in the corner. Abby and Callum sit five tables away with their baby girl in a high chair between them, cooing as she smashes a Nutella pancake all over her chubby little cheeks.

Casey is beautiful. I'd love a daughter one day, a little girl that grows into a friend. Abby's parents gaze in admiration from across the table at their first grandchild. Hard to believe this sweet little granny is the same woman that tore strips off the manager in the carpark not twenty-four hours earlier.

'Emma, don't sit on your own, join us.' Abby waves me over enthusiastically. I shake my head feeling like a spare part. Thankfully Karen, Fran and Kerry rock up, saving me any more singleton embarrassment. They couldn't have timed it better.

'How's the head, Kerry?' Abby asks as the waitress ushers us to a bigger table so we can all eat together.

'Jesus, girls, I'm telling you that blue stuff is lethal.' Kerry's face is paper-white. Last night's mascara is smudged into the creases below her eyes.

'You'll have to stick to the green one tonight,' I tease. 'Sea Breeze, I think it's called.'

'Sea Heave more like.' Kerry puts a hand over her mouth and swallows hard.

'Anyone up for some sightseeing this morning?' I'd spotted some photos of the old town in a brochure in the reception, and I'm a secret history buff. I love the rich insight into the past, the thought of millions of others pacing the streets before us. I also relish the idea of being nowhere near Eddie Harrington semi-naked by the pool.

'You've got to be joking me.' Kerry slumps forward, cradling her head in her hands. 'I'm going straight back to bed after this.'

'That's a great start to the holiday. What about you, Karen? Fran?' I can tell it's a non-runner by the way they glance coyly at each other over their coffees. Yuck. And it's not because they're gay. It's simply because I have no one that looks at me like that.

'Abs what about you?' It's a last resort. I already know she'll be busy with wedding stuff.

'I can't, sweetie, I'm so sorry. We are meeting the wedding planner this morning to finalise things before the big day.'

'No worries.' I take a mouthful of scalding hot coffee and hope the burn takes away the other pang I feel, the all too familiar pang of loneliness.

We go our separate ways, arranging to meet by the pool later in the afternoon. I stroll to reception, trying to ignore that broadening hole in my heart, wishing I had someone to share this with. Will I ever find the right man, one I can be myself around, and don't apparently terrify? In Dublin, when I'm working, I don't usually have time to feel lonely. An idle mind can be dangerous.

As I sift through a few scattered tourist brochures placed in a Perspex display, a rush of warm breath tickles the back of my neck, sending a shiver rippling through the length of my spine. Startled, I jolt around and take a step back.

Eddie towers above me, looking ridiculously good in a tight white T-shirt and navy cargo shorts.

'What are you doing here? Are you following me?'

'Don't be so paranoid. I'm heading into the old town to see the ruins. What are you doing?' His familiar aftershave envelops me. I should tell him to beat it. I don't want him getting the wrong idea, but a sightseeing companion would be nice. At the very least, it might prevent me from getting mugged on the street or approached by random men wanting to draw a portrait of me, like the time I visited Paris.

I hesitate for a second, stepping from one foot to the other before admitting, 'I'm heading that way anyway. I suppose you can tag along. Don't get any big ideas, though.'

'I wouldn't dream of it.' His smile reaches all the way to the crinkling corners of his eyes. 'I thought you'd be sunning yourself at the beach or the pool.'

'I will be later.'

'Now that would be a sight worth seeing.'

'Eddie, please, enough fooling around.'

He shrugs and offers that lopsided smile again before asking the receptionist to call us a taxi. When it arrives, I sit in the front, determined to reinstate a little distance between us. The driver drops us at the Pile Gate, as shown on the tourist map. The sandy coloured architecture is gothic, majestic, and terribly romantic.

'Did you watch *Game of Thrones*?' I breathe it all in, revelling in the sheer magnificence of our surroundings, temporarily forgetting Eddie is *The One That Got Away*.

'Of course. Who didn't?' He smiles at me. 'If you could be any character in the entire eight seasons, who would you be?'

I consider my answer as we begin a slow stroll, companionably admiring the ruins, the sun deliciously kissing my face, heating me through to the bones.

'Hmm, would I rather have been sleeping with my arrogant but loyal twin, murdered by my heroic, self-sacrificing lover/nephew, or the viciously violated, but still living to fight another day, Queen of the North?'

'When you put it like that.' Eddie laughs and runs a hand over a line of dark stubble. He is poster pin-up good looking, even with that broken nose. An image of him on a poster for my new skincare range flashes through my mind. His face would look phenomenal on a billboard. I brush the thought away and clear my throat, taking the time to form my answer.

'In all honesty, it's easy. I'd be Daenerys Targaryen any day. Her growth and strength throughout was admirable, the way she was sold to the Dothraki King, yet managed to not only fall in love with him but make him fall in love with her... She was beautiful too, which helps, I suppose.'

'She was, if you're in to the white-haired look. I prefer brunettes myself, particularly ones with striking emerald eyes and a penchant for romance novels.' Eddie glances sideways at me with a deep resounding chuckle. I lean closer to allow room for an approaching couple to pass by and my arm brushes against his. Fine hairs on my body immediately stand to attention, but I ignore his flirtatious comments.

'And who would you be if you could be any character?' I focus on the background noise, the passing tourists and locals, anything other than the sensation of his hot skin brushing against mine.

'Honestly?' He arches a thick eyebrow. 'I wouldn't be anyone else in the world right now – dead or alive, historical or fictional,' he pauses for a second, and I wait for some cheesy chat-up line to fall from his lips.

'That night...'

We stop in front of an enormous round fountain intricately carved with masks that dribble trickling water into a shallow pool below.

'I told you yesterday, leave the past in the past.'

'What if I don't want to?' His strong arms fold across his chest, and I battle not to stare at the veins of his bulging biceps, the very same biceps that I had clung onto ecstatically as he drove into me. I blink hard and force away the vivid, multicoloured memories.

'You had your chance. Now drop it, you're ruining my ruins experience. If you want to get in my good books, buy me an ice-cream and stop talking shite.'

Eddie laughs and shakes his head, strolling to a nearby hut to stand in line. My eyes fixate on his broad back and perfectly rounded bum.

He's clearly on the rebound. Now Maria has finished with him, he's looking to fill the gap. I'd have to be very careful not to let my guard down for a second. Because if I do, my body will betray me, and Eddie Harrington will use me and discard me like he did before. And he was hard enough to get over the first time.

CHAPTER ELEVEN

EDDIE

I take a chance on what flavour ice-cream she might like, remembering the sweet stash in her handbag. If the way she licks at it is anything to go by, lemon sherbet is the way to her heart. We sit at Onofrio's Fountain while we eat. Emma stares at the architecture. I stare at her.

Why didn't I call her after everything? That little voice inside, the devil on my shoulder, whispers the painfully accurate answer into my subconscious. I was ashamed. Because I can't undo what I've done. Because I can never take back what happened the day that I left her house.

'You've gone quiet, Eddie.' She glances at me, a thoughtful look creasing her face.

'I thought you'd be happy with the peace.'

'Look, our friends are marrying each other. Maybe we can be friends?' She's close enough for me to take note of the hundreds of golden flecks dancing in her irises.

'Sure.' I shrug as she shoots me down again. I want to be more than her friend. And the more I think about it, the more I want it. If the last year has taught me anything, it's to take nothing for granted. Tomorrow is promised to none of us.

We stroll the length of the main street, or Stradun as it's called in the tourist maps. Tiny gift shops offer souvenirs. Midday approaches, the heat of the sun is almost unbearable, the dampness starts to show on my T-shirt under my arms. The prospect of a cool swim is particularly enticing now.

'Want to head back to the hotel?' If it sounds like a pick-up line, she doesn't take it that way.

'Good idea.'

We flag a taxi outside the city gate. She slides into the back seat with me this time, maybe I am making progress after all. I instinctively lift my hand to take hers; it hovers mid-air before flopping down again. I want to walk before I can run.

As we arrive back at the reception, I keep my head down and my feet moving, for fear she might suggest I check if my own suite is available. If it is, then I'll have to move out, which sofa or no sofa, I don't intend to do.

Back at room 425, the maid has done the rounds. The bed is made, fresh rose petals scattered on the Egyptian cotton sheets, and new bottles of water replace the ones we drank. I flop onto the couch and look at Emma, a small frown burrowing on my brows.

'What are we doing now?' I'm pushing my luck.

'*I* am going to find my friends at the pool and order something to eat.'

'Huh. I thought they were *our* friends?'

She attempts to arrange her features into a grimace, but her lips are definitely twitching. I'm almost sure she's fighting a smirk. She pretends to be unaffected by me, but I remember how her body trembled underneath mine, how she cried out my name and dug her nails into my back while I moved inside her. My tongue runs over my lips at the memory. I swear she's thinking about it too. Either way, I'm going to remind her.

'And, I thought we were friends?' I stand up, close the distance between us, and deliberately remove my T-shirt, silently, daring her to look at my exposed torso. She seemed to like it this morning. She point blank refuses to take her eyes from mine, but her small swallow doesn't go unnoticed.

'Eddie, why do you insist on taking your clothes off in front of me?' She takes a step back from me, increasing the distance between us.

'I'm getting ready for the pool.' I don't even try and hide my grin. 'Friends see each other without clothes on all the time, right?'

'Friends don't deliberately play games with each other.' Her gaze wavers momentarily, and she looks to the floor.

'It's not my fault if you like what you see.' Arrogant, maybe, direct definitely.

'Two can play that game, you know.' Emma arches an eyebrow and raises her hand to the straps of that white dress.

My heart lodges in my throat, practically winding me. She wouldn't, would she?

She drops one strap at first, exposing a tanned shoulder and the silky skin of her upper chest. Glancing up at me from under those long dark eyelashes, she checks she has my attention. Oh my god, does she have my attention. She lets the other strap down, and the dress slips, revealing an inch of her full, tanned cleavage. My shorts bulge at the sight. So much for me playing by myself.

She shimmies the dress further down with a wiggle that sends more blood rushing below. A white strapless bikini supports beautiful, full breasts. I take an involuntary step to close the final foot between us. My arms instinctively lift but freeze mid-air.

'It's not my fault if you like what you see,' she says, playfully stepping back before I can even think of putting my hands anywhere near her. A tiny ripple of laughter echoes around the room, and she turns away from me, pulls on one of those flimsy beach kaftan things around herself and drops the dress completely.

Fuck. That was hot. There's no way I'm leaving this bedroom willingly. I don't mean right now. I mean for the duration of this holiday. I only hope Mrs Queenan has a few more unexpected guests up her sleeve.

Emma has other ideas. 'I wonder if your room is available yet.'

It's like she can read my fucking mind.

'Hmm.' I root through my holdall to find a pair of swimming shorts. Just as I'm considering dropping everything right this second to put them on, Emma grabs a small beach bag and waltzes past me.

'I'll meet you by the pool, my friend.' She blows me a kiss and laughs again as she breezes out the door.

CHAPTER TWELVE

EMMA

The infinity pool creates the illusion of being at the edge of the sea, though it's a relief to observe the sturdy looking glass wall securing its far side. I find a free lounger and glance around for any sign of the others. I don't recognise anyone bar Abby's younger sister, Alicia, lying a few metres away on her back, snoozing in the sunshine.

Several couples lounge nearby, reading or scrolling through their phones, probably teasing their co-workers at home with the obligatory pictures of their tanned feet. A waiter passes by, and I order a club sandwich and mojito. Removing my phone from my satchel, I notice two missed calls from my mother and a text from Sarah. My mother never calls for a simple chat. Has she heard about my latest break-up? My eyes roll into my head at the thought of listening to the 'when I was your age, I was married with three children speech' again.

She'd love to plan my big white wedding to impress her snobby friends, the ladies that lunch; Rita, Sheila and Breege.

I'm a permanent source of disappointment to her, and them for that matter. I've never been able to connect with my mother in the way that daughters are supposed to. I wasn't brought up smothered with kisses and cuddles. Maybe that's why I've been searching for love ever since I left home, why I devour every romance novel I can get my hands on, because I've never experienced any real form of it myself. I've had boyfriends, even thought I was in love before, but it inevitably fizzled out, amounting to nothing more than a passing infatuation.

My mother assured me that hairdressing and make-up would get me nowhere in life. She was almost right; my first two salons nearly bankrupted me. I didn't know enough about business, but I ploughed on anyway, thinking I could make up the difference with passion, overspending on stock and under-booking clients. I was determined to prove her wrong, to make something of myself in my own right. The more she belittled the salon, the more time and energy I invested into it, determined to prove her wrong.

After my initial sharp learning curve, I combined the hair and beauty into a one-stop shop for everything, halved the overheads and doubled the profits. I was as surprised as anyone when the Jervis Shopping Centre salon became a goldmine. Once I got a taste of success, I opened a second branch on the south side of Dublin, then a third in Liffey Valley. I won awards, became featured in some of the Irish glossy magazines, yet still, my mother refused to congratulate me or even acknowledge my achievements. My fourth salon in Blackrock failed to impress her, despite the celebrity clientele it attracts. Stella Holmes, vlogger and celebrity influencer, regularly posts about my Blackrock salon on her Instagram.

I'm hoping the new spa will be too successful for even my mother to ignore; bigger, fancier, more luxurious than anything before it, complete with four hydrotherapy suites and the best seaweed baths money can buy. Every single person who walks through the door will be desperate to purchase something from my new exclusive skincare range as a souvenir of their wonderful experience, including her snooty lunch buddies.

It's kind of pathetic that I still dream of making her proud, that I continuously seek that validation, but for some reason, there's still a little freckly ten-year-old girl inside of me that longs for it. Though apparently, no matter how many businesses I open, I won't be deemed a success in her eyes until I'm a respectably married woman like her.

With a niggle of apprehension in my stomach, I hit the voicemail button, pressing the phone tightly to my ear, whilst watching the sun glistening off the crystal clear water of the pool.

'Emma, it's me. I need to talk to you. Call me back.'

She probably wants to set me up with Andy The Accountant, Rita's eternally single son and the most boring man that ever walked the earth, unless you're into prehistoric coins and illegal metal detecting on private property after dark. I throw the phone into my bag, before remembering I didn't read Sarah's message, and retrieve it again.

Outbid again :(

Someone means business, but so do I.

I swallow down the niggle of irritation at whoever is putting themselves between me and my path to success. If I could get my hands on the culprit standing in the way of my progress, there's no telling what I'd be liable to do to them. I type a quick text.

Leave it until tomorrow. Still a couple of days left, and we don't want to drive the price out of our reach. We need to box clever. Sleep on it and put a bid in at nine tomorrow morning. Keep me posted.

I throw the phone down next to me as the waiter returns with my drink, ice bounces against the fresh mint, and condensation glistens on the outside of the glass.

'Another lovely day.' He's a smiley man in his fifties. He hovers, but in a kind manner.

'British?' he asks. His English is exceptionally good.

'Irish.'

'Lovely. My wife always wanted to go to Ireland. Just give me a shout if you need anything.' He offers a toothy smile and leaves me to my own thoughts.

Slipping off my kaftan, I apply factor thirty, pushing all thoughts of my mother and work to the back of my mind. I haven't been on holiday all year, and I am determined nothing will spoil this week for me. I smother my chest, arms and legs with the coconut-scented lotion. My skin's naturally tanned, but I'm not used to this heat.

'Need a hand?' Eddie materialises out of thin air again. He looks indecently decent in a pair of turquoise swimming shorts and nothing else. Half of the people around the pool are checking him out; the other half are asleep.

I try not to gawp at his perfectly defined abs, six perfect symmetrical squares, neater than the contents of a Mr Kipling cake box, and equally as mouth-watering.

Does he realise what he's doing to me? Yes, of course he does; it's part of his game plan. I need him gone before I do something I'll regret.

'Did you check if your room is ready yet?'

'What's the rush? It's great being able to spend some time with an old friend.' Winking at me, his eyes then roam over my body in a way that is anything other than friendly. He takes the bottle of sun cream from my hands. I contemplate stopping him, but the thought of his touch is secretly thrilling. I'm enslaved in this will I/won't I give into him bubble. My head says no way, my heart screams he'll break it.

But my lady parts scream the loudest. I'm teetering on the edge.

He squirts a dollop of cream into his huge hands and sits behind me, one leg on either side of the sunlounger, securing me in position between his thighs. I hold my breath in anticipation of the touch of his hands. He gently brushes my loose hair to the side and begins kneading the knots in my shoulders. Strong hands massage the cream into my sensitive skin, rubbing in a circular motion, fingers pressing tightly into my bare back.

'You're tense. Relax. I promise you're in safe hands,' he says lowly into my ear. As he leans forward, his hot torso rests temptingly against my skin.

'I'm about as safe as a baby seal being circled by a hungry shark.' My breath is heavy, throaty. I swallow hard, but I'm unable to stop him. He squirts more lotion into his hands, and I'm relieved that he hasn't yet finished. I'm enjoying this so much more than what is good for me.

His hands extend lower, towards the base of my spine, and he works his way around to my waist. My insides contract into a big ball of burning longing. Goosebumps ripple across my skin, every tiny hair on my body stands to attention.

'Chilly, Emma?' I hear the smile in his smug, defiant tone.

Eddie is loving this. Hands trace over my stomach. I glance around to see if anyone we know is in the vicinity to witness this frankly pornographic scene. I've never been as grateful for my oversized sunglasses. His hands inch upwards, stroking the underwiring of my bikini top. I freeze at where his fingers are heading. 'Can't have you getting any tan lines now, can we?' His tone is almost jovial as his fingers skirt underneath my breasts.

Every single cell in my body is on fire, silently begging Eddie Harrington to quench the flames. My muscle memory remembers exactly what he is capable of.

'You two look very cosy!' Abby's sudden arrival startles me, and I jump, causing Eddie to snigger. He pats me on the back and falls back onto his own sunlounger, face down, I notice. Is he trying to hide his own interest? Or is this simply another game? Torment Emma and watch her spontaneously combust with lust. I might have won the first round, but he definitely won the second. How many more games will I be dragged into before one of us calls time?

Abby throws her towel down on the sunlounger next to mine, the grin on her face extends to her ears and I doubt it has anything to do with her upcoming nuptials. My cheeks flush, at being caught enjoying Eddie's hands sliding up and down the length of me.

'How did you get on this morning?' I ask her, hoping to distract her from the almost-sex show.

'Grand. All set. A minor issue with the florist, but nothing that couldn't be fixed.'

'Where's Callum?' Eddie asks.

'Casey is napping, so he's gone back to bed with her. I thought I'd catch a few rays and enjoy the peace while I can. It's so rare these days.' Abby throws her dress on the back of her lounger, revealing a gorgeous cerise bikini and a body that doesn't look like it's birthed a baby. She has the enviable ability to eat what she likes without putting on a single pound! What I wouldn't do for a metabolism like that. Where she is slim, I'm more curvy. Mind you, the lemon sherbets don't help.

The waiter brings my sandwich over and places the plate on a tiny rattan table between myself and Eddie, who helps himself to half. 'Can we get two more of these, please?' he asks the waiter.

'What?' He looks at me, a cheeky golden glint reflecting in his irises. 'Sharing's caring, right?' He's crossed every physical boundary now, short of using my toothbrush, and for all I know, he could have done that too. The quicker he gets his own room, the better.

'You know, guys, I'm so glad I bumped into you.' Abby has a look of innocence on her face, but an obvious devilment shines through her twinkling chocolate eyes. I have a feeling she's looking for something, and whatever it is, I'm not going to like it. A babysitter, perhaps? I'm no good with kids; she should know that by now. I like them, I'd love my own, but as of yet, I simply don't know how to relate to them.

'What is it?' I sigh, but she knows I'll do pretty much whatever she asks. Perk of her being the bride.

'James and Nadine are flying in today last minute, and as you know, there is limited availability here...' I groan internally as her smile widens.

James O'Malley is Callum's best friend. They didn't know if he'd be able to make it because Nadine's father was sick, but seemingly he's well enough now for them to fly out. I know what she's going to ask of me. Doesn't she realise it's killing me, being in Eddie's presence? Especially because I seem to have accidentally forgotten rule 101, how he rejected me, and that he always goes back to Maria in the end.

'That's fantastic they're able to make it. It was destroying James that he might not be able to.' From the grin emerging on his face, Eddie knows exactly where this is going.

'So, would you guys mind terribly being roommates for another couple of nights? I promise as soon as there is a free room, it will be yours, Eddie.' Abby looks at him with those deep doe-like eyes; there's not a man or a woman in the world that could refuse her.

'No problem at all,' Eddies replies smoothly, as if he's taking one for the team. Argh. With the tingling sensation left on my skin from his erotic sunscreen application, I can't promise not to give him one.

CHAPTER THIRTEEN

EDDIE

Marcus, Ollie and Nathan have arrived, and happily disturb the peace by throwing a rugby ball violently around the pool. 'Get in, you big pansy!' Marcus calls to me. I have the perfect spot, sitting two feet away from Emma, the last thing I want to do is lose it, but my idiotic teammates need to be taught a lesson. I leap off my lounger and dive-bomb into the pool straight in front of Marcus, covering him in a riptide of water, before snatching the ball from his wet hands.

'Butter fingers.' I swim past him, knowing he won't be able to resist following.

A game of water rugby ensues, only there's no ref and no rules. We splash several sunbathers in the process, and a couple shoot us a look of disgust as they gather their belongings and leave. Like the playground days, I find myself constantly glancing at Emma to see if she's watching me, but she has her nose buried in that pink book again, or at least she's making a better job of pretending to read it than she managed yesterday.

Callum arrives at the pool with the baby strapped to him in a sling, crying, a full bottle of milk in his hand. Fatherhood suits him. He makes the baby look like the coolest accessory a guy can have. A ripple of envy washes over me again. I love kids, probably because I'm a big one myself. Their simple nature and honest approach appeal to me. We function on the same wavelength.

Abby sits up with a sigh, as Callum takes the baby out of the sling to hand her over. She barely got twenty minutes. I throw the ball as hard as I can at Marcus's shiny head, which reflects the sunlight like a mirror, and pull myself out of the pool.

'Abby, I'll take her for you.' I dry myself quickly with a towel, throw it down and walk purposefully towards them. Abby's eyes widen in disbelief, eyebrows raised at my outstretched arms.

'Trust me, I've done this a hundred times before.' A doubtful look crosses Abby's face, but she dubiously hands the child over. I take the bottle and return to my own sunlounger with the crying child, not oblivious to the fact that Emma is staring at me, her full lips forming a perfect O in surprise.

I position the child in the crook of my arm, not so flat that she can't see, and tease the bottle into her tiny mouth, twisting it in a small circle until she latches on. Innocent topaz eyes stare curiously up at me, and I can't help but grin down at the little beauty. Keira has four kids, and Matthew has three. In our family, you are handed a child the minute you walk through someone's front door. I'm no stranger to changing nappies or burping babies.

Callum drags a parasol over to shade us, and Casey grips my index finger as she vigorously sucks the bottle.

'Would you look at the baby whisperer!' Emma doesn't attempt to hide the shock in her voice.

'I love kids. We have the same IQ. I can't wait to have my own one day.' I glance up at her to see a fleeting look of what I think might be admiration cross her face, and she smiles, placing her book down as she watches closely. Abby seems reassured that her pride and joy is being taken good care of, and resumes her position on the recliner. Callum flops down next to her, unstraps the sling and gives me a thumbs up. The once large scar on his chest has faded into an angry pink line, another reminder of how fragile life can be.

As Casey drinks, I speak to her in a quiet sing-song voice. 'You are going to break some hearts when you are older. Your daddy better buy a big gun to keep the boys away. Don't worry, Uncle Eddie will mind you.' I'm showing off. I can't help it, but now I have Emma's attention, it's an opportunity to show her I could be so much more than just the man who didn't call her, if only she'd let me. In fact, I'm so determined to prove it to her that even I am starting to truly believe it. I had a bad run of it, but things will get better. They have to, I'll make sure of it.

The rest of Abby's friends arrive at the pool, the little one, Kerry, looking a bit worse for wear after last night's finale of tequila slammers by all accounts.

'Hooker Harrington, you surprise us all.' The one with the hairband is openly shocked. I flinch at the sound of my nickname flowing from her tongue. Somehow it seems less harsh when it comes from the lads' mouths. I'm not really a hooker, but was definitely a little promiscuous when I was younger. The thought of settling down never frightened me, only now I'm actually frightened for the woman that has to put up with me, truth be known.

My mind wanders to my own nephews and niece, who will soon be my new neighbours, with any luck. I can't wait to have them home, even though the circumstances aren't ideal. Matt would have preferred to stay in the States, but it's just so much more practical to be around family now, after everything. The marketing company he worked for can't keep him on in his current condition. He and his family need help. I'm going to make sure they get it. Starting by kitting out their new house with everything and anything that makes their lives easier.

The old regret starts to creep in, invading my brain and body like an army of invisible crawling ants. The demon on my shoulder whispers menacingly into my ear, how dare I be happy? How dare I be here, enjoying myself, after everything?

I swallow hard and shun the dark thoughts. At least by buying the house for them, I'm giving them something back. Nothing will make up for what I took, but the house is a practical help.

'You okay?' Emma frowns at me. She must have been watching me closer than I realised.

'Grand.' I force away the negativity that threatens to consume me. 'Want a cuddle?' I meant the baby, but wouldn't be averse to one myself.

'You're doing a great job there yourself,' she says, as I sit the baby up, and she lets out an almighty croaking burp. Laughter ripples around the pool, and I find myself smiling, momentarily distracted once again from that heaviness squeezing at my heart.

CHAPTER FOURTEEN

EMMA

Twilight etches its way in, the scorching sun sinking into the enchanting Adriatic Sea. Perfect, fluffy clouds appear super-imposed against the bright coral sky. Calvin Harris drifts from carefully positioned speakers around the pool, and almost anyone that's not one of us has got up and left. If the highly competitive poolside rugby wasn't enough to send them running, the tipsy adult banter of our gathering crowd certainly was.

Kerry, Karen and Fran laze behind me with their second jug of Sea Heave. Marcus, Ollie, Eddie and Nathan sit to my left, sipping bottles of Corona. Abby lies on a rattan sunbed between Callum's legs, with their baby girl sleeping on her chest. They look like a poster advert for a family holiday. If Thomas Cook are looking for a replacement for Jamie and Louise, they need look no further.

I had intended to go back to the room, shower, change and put on a fresh face of make-up, but I'm having too much fun to move. Surrounded by my oldest friends and some new ones too, I feel more at home here tonight than I sometimes do in my newly refurbished, but sometimes lonely, house.

The message tone from my phone sounds on the sunlounger four feet away from me.

'Do you need this?' Karen holds it up.

'Who is it?'

Karen gasps, then hoots with laughter, pressing her hands over her widening eyes, before peeking again. 'Emma Elizabeth Harvey, who on earth is sending you dick pics? And not just one, but an entire fucking collage of them! My, oh my. Is that the same guy? Or is it nine different dicks? Jesus, Mary and feckin' Joseph. I can't take it.'

'It's wasted on you, Ellen!' Kerry squeals, snatching the phone out of Karen's hands. Ellen became Karen's new nickname the second she came out. It's an 'in' joke in our group, and not malicious in any way.

'Give it to me. I haven't seen anything like it in a long time,' Kerry demands. Her boyfriend, Craig, is in the army; he's away a lot. Apparently, he doesn't send dick pics. In fact he barely seems to text or call at all, now I come to think of it.

Eddie glances over from the sunlounger next to me. His eyebrows knit together for a split second then he looks away. Alicia has left her lounger and chooses this precise moment to splash him from the middle of the pool. She flicks her caramel-coloured hair around in an attempt to get his attention, and a stab of panic assaults my stomach.

'It can only be from Holly. Tinder has a lot to answer for. That's the fifth one this week.' I roll my eyes, wave the phone away and take a sip of my cocktail.

'Holly is my kind of girl.' Kerry's tone is approving.

I glance sideways, looking for Eddie, eternally conscious of his proximity, but he's disappeared. Shit. Maybe he's snuck off with Alicia? A stab of jealousy knifes my stomach. I put my glass down and lean further forward to squint behind the safety of my sunglasses. I turned him down. If he's looking for a rebound shag, he's clearly not short of options. Abby mentioned she broke up with her boyfriend a few months back, and no one in the entire world could blame the girl for making a pass at Eddie.

The sensation of hands around my ankles startles me, as I realise all too late what's happening. The high pitched squeal that escapes my mouth is unrecognisable even to me, as my bum hits the water with an ungracious slap. Just before my head is completely submerged, firm hands grab my waist and hoist me up onto strong, broad shoulders. I look down to find my legs are wrapped around Eddie's neck, just not quite perhaps how I'd been imagining.

'Who's for a bit of pool volleyball?' Eddie calls to our friends as I straighten my sunglasses on my head and attempt to regain some kind of composure. I should be mad as hell that he dunked me, but all I feel is stupidly flattered, when not ten seconds earlier, Alicia blatantly threw another subliminal offer on the table.

Warm hands reach up to lock my thighs securely in position, steadying me from a potential fall. Oh, I'm in danger of falling, alright.

I place my hands on top of his, telling myself it's for added security, but I know the truth – I'm staking a silent claim, and he is actively encouraging it.

The boisterous chatter from our group quietens as everyone watches us. Karen shoots me a knowing look, and I shrug in an inevitable gesture. If the striptease didn't get me earlier, the way he cradled the baby was my undoing. There has been no mention of Maria, he's barely left my side all day, and his phone hasn't rang once…maybe, just maybe, it really is over?

'I'd love to, but I'm kind of caught where I am.' Callum

gestures to his baby girl and soon to be wife, using him like a memory foam mattress.

'Marcus?' Eddie spins us round, tightening his grip on my thighs.

'Nah, I don't wanna get my hair wet.' Marcus runs a hand over his bald head and flashes a toothy grin. 'I've got a better idea – another game, one that everyone can play.'

'Go on,' Callum urges, though Marcus needs minimal encouragement by the look of it.

'Truth or dare.' He swigs a mouthful of his frothy pint of lager and smacks his lips together.

'Oh, I love truth or dare.' Kerry squeals, rubbing her hands together. 'Can I start?'

Eddie walks us to the side of the pool, helps me slide from his shoulders, over his wide, wet back and back into the sitting position he stole me from. My skin prickles as it rubs deliciously against his. Heat spreads from my stomach to my breasts. He hauls himself up out of the pool and sits next to me, shaking his wet hair at the girls like a damp dog, laughing as they shriek obscenities at him.

'Truth or dare? What are we? Like fourteen, guys? Seriously?' Eddie protests, his forehead creases with three tiny lines, and he runs a thumb over his scar.

'Chill out, Harrington. I promise we won't ask who stole your cherry. It'll be fun,' Callum says.

'Okay, Abby, you first. Truth or dare?' Kerry picks on the bride-to-be.

'Hmm. I guess it will have to be truth because I can't exactly do anything too daring right now.' Her eyes return to the sleeping baby on her chest. She runs a finger lightly over her gorgeous chubby cheek.

'Ah. There's nothing I couldn't ask you that I don't already know, is there?' Kerry considers it for a second.

'Well, don't ask me something that my fiancé doesn't

already know if you want a wedding in a few days' time,' she jokes, but there's a hint of warning in her words. Abby's always been great at talking about other people's private lives, heck she makes a good living out of it, but she's not nearly as open when it comes to her own personal life.

'I have it,' Karen says. She leans into Kerry's ear and whispers something which results in Kerry's spluttering giggle.

'Where's the naughtiest place you ever had sex?' Karen nudges me and winks. We already know the answer, but it will give Marcus food for thought. Abby colours slightly and mouths 'bitches' with a shake of her head.

Callum sniggers. 'Go on, hon, tell them.'

Abby shrugs and says, 'Marcus's Audi.'

'Fuck off. Ye dirty bastards!' Marcus's face screws up in distaste. He shakes his head and downs the remainder of his bottle, signalling the waiter to bring more. 'When? Actually, I don't want to know. I hope you wiped the seats down afterwards, you rotten feckers. My daughters sit on those seats. Jesus, I haven't even banged Shelly in it.'

Laughter ripples around the pool.

'Okay, I've heard enough.' Marcus raises a hand to signify the end of that conversation.

'It's my turn to pick, seeing as I had to answer,' Abby says, that devious twinkle reappearing in her eyes as she reshuffles the baby so she can sit up a little straighter.

'Eddie, truth or dare?' Abby says, as Callum whispers something into her ear, and she giggles like a schoolgirl.

Eddie shifts uncomfortably from one butt cheek to the other while he decides. His usual easy demeanour is replaced with the same burrowing of his eyebrows I witnessed earlier. He's not happy. I thought this would be right up his street after his performance in the suite earlier. Then it hits me. It's not a dare he's worried about, it's the truth. What has he got to hide?

'Dare.' He confirms my suspicions. Whatever Callum said about there being more to him than we know, he certainly appears to be concealing something beneath his overly confident surface.

'I was hoping you'd say that.' Abby grins and flicks her hair back from her face. Eddie lets out a low groan.

Maybe she'll make him sing a song. Or take his clothes off. Or is that just wishful thinking on my behalf?

'I dare you to kiss Emma,' she states with an air of authority. 'And I mean really kiss her. Like you mean it.' She rubs her hands together, like Cilla Black her-fucking-self.

'Oh, that's something I think we'd all love to see – *again*.' Marcus rubs his hands together gleefully.

'Abby, that's not fair! It's supposed to be Eddie's dare, not mine!' I protest, but my tone isn't as offended as it could be. Between the escalating chemistry, the cocktails and the threat of another woman, it doesn't sound like the worst idea in the world. Though I'm under no illusion I might feel differently tomorrow.

'If you do it, we'll let you off this round, Emma,' Kerry adds in with an inconspicuous wink.

'This is a conspiracy, guys. Come on! You all know we've been there done that.' I don't even try to deny it.

'Exactly. We think you have some unfinished business, and we'd like to see that it gets finished, once and for all,' Abby says, with an ever-widening smile.

Eddie is oddly silent. Did I read him wrong? Maybe he's noticed how awful my naked skin looks and had second thoughts? His teasing, flirting with me, could just have been a game all along. Now he's being forced to act on it, he might not want to. A heavy anticipation crushes my sternum.

Before I know what's happening, he swivels me towards him and gazes at me with those intensely engaging darkening pupils.

'Emma, I'm really sorry about this.' His lips inch towards mine, hands cupping my hips loosely. His intentions are clear. Shit, he's going to do this. Right here, in front of our friends.

'Actually, if I'm totally honest, I'm not.' His gravelly voice is low enough that only I can hear him.

It's gone oddly quiet, but even as I'm drowning in Eddie's blackening eyes, I feel everyone else's focussed on us. My face angles towards his, an involuntary automatic response. The last year melts away; it's just him and me, like it was that first night. With open eyes, his lips touch mine, tentatively at first, his warm breath rushes into my mouth. I can't tear my stare from his. He's beautiful. I want to watch him, even as I taste him.

Shocked at my own lack of inhibition, fire rips violently through my core. My lips tingle, my tongue searches for his, deepening our kiss. My hands have a mind of their own, reaching for his chest, fingertips tracing the lines of his perfect pecs. His formidable hands move to my back, pulling me closer, pushing my chest against his, skin on skin as his tongue licks and dances with mine. A hot wave of longing floods through me. His kiss is excruciatingly addictive, it's never going to be enough. I pull away abruptly while I'm still able. Only then do I look away.

'Fucking hell, you guys have got it going on. That was better than the dick pic!' Kerry applauds, and Abby wolf whistles, forgetting the sleeping child on top of her.

'I'll tell you something, Harrington, you might have lost your wingman,' Marcus nods at Callum, 'but by Christ you've gained the best fucking wingwoman on god's green earth.'

Eddie takes my hand and kisses it before whispering, 'Are we done playing games now?'

I shrug, unable to trust the words that might fall out of my mouth. I've got a feeling Eddie Harrington might just get the first second chance that I've ever given.

CHAPTER FIFTEEN

EDDIE

The fun has rapidly evaporated from our private lust-fuelled games. Emma's been lurking in the back of my mind for an entire year, so this is not exactly a surprising development. I glance around, wondering how quickly I can get her out of here, back to our room. She wants this as much as I do; she communicated it clearly, as her tongue stroked mine. But I know if we do this, there will be no going back, because I can't promise to stay away from her again, even if she does deserve better.

The waiter returns to ask if anyone needs a refill. Emma asks Marcus if he'd prefer a truth or dare, but I can't focus on their exchange. My mind is finely tuned to Emma's minuscule, micro-body movements. The way she readjusts her cleavage in her wet bikini top, how she wiggles her bum on the paving underneath it, leaving her legs open that tiny bit wider in the process and consequently resting the skin of her thigh against mine. She flicks her hair from her shoulder and glances at me with a smirk. She's the most practised flirt I've ever met, and it only adds to her appeal.

I tune back into the conversation as Marcus stands and pulls down his shorts, showing us way too much of his anatomy, although the entire team has seen it hundreds of times already. He should seriously consider a bit of manscaping. He's like a hairier version of Shrek. How Shelly puts up with him is beyond me.

He kicks off his shorts with the grace of an angry bear and legs it towards the beach for a skinny dip. A woman in her fifties hangs on to her husband's arms as Marcus flies past them, belting out the Irish national anthem at the top of his loquacious lungs. Emma, Abby and Karen shake, howling with laughter. I tut and send up a silent prayer that no one recognises us, as a passing tourist on the beach takes out a phone to film him. If this goes viral, Coach will kill us.

Marcus returns a few minutes later, at the same time as the very disturbed looking waiter with more drinks. Just as Marcus wraps a towel around his waist, he is shoved into the pool from behind by Callum's younger brother, Mark, who has just arrived from Dubai.

'Little fecker!' Marcus emerges from the water shaking his fist, but he's laughing. He approaches Mark and shakes his hand. 'I wondered when you'd show up.'

The handshake is a vigorous one, as Marcus then pushes Mark, fully clothed, into the pool. Mark scrambles out of the water, spluttering.

'I suppose I asked for that.' Mark shrugs good-naturedly, and Marcus throws him a dry towel just as Callum's older brother, Brian, arrives.

'Bid the women goodbye now. It's time for the stag night,' Mark says with a devious glint in his bright blue eyes. Stag? They have got to be joking! We had that last month in Amsterdam. I'm just beginning to make a little progress with

Emma, now they're expecting me to leave her. My heart drops to my stomach.

Abby groans but shifts her weight off Callum, pushing him up from his position on the recliner. 'I thought we'd gotten this over with! Bring him back in one piece, and that includes his eyebrows.'

'Don't worry, Abby, I'll mind him for you.' Mark grins.

'That's what worries me.'

'Actually, Abby, we have our own fun planned.' Alicia, Abby's sister winks knowingly. 'Hen night!' she shrieks like an excited child.

I discreetly run a finger up over the length of Emma's spine, revelling in the resulting goosebumps raising over her silky skin. I'm determined to leave a lasting impression. 'I'll see you later.' I brush my lips deliberately against her earlobe before I stand.

'You will.' She bites her lower lip in a promising fashion.

'Okay, lads, let's get this done.' The quicker we do this, the quicker we can go to bed. And I don't mean to sleep. I have no intention of spending another night on Emma's couch.

'Shower and reconvene at the reception area in thirty minutes?' Brian suggests, eyeing our swimming togs with a frown.

An hour later, we're gathered around a roulette table in an enormous private games suite in the hotel penthouse. It's been transformed into a casino for the occasion. Croupiers stand at various tables, ready to assist. Cocktail servers strut the length and breadth of the room, handing out crystal tumblers containing expensive golden liquor. In the far corner of the room, a burlesque dancer, wearing only black nipple tassels, stockings and something very flimsy in between, sings a low sexy version of an Amy Winehouse song as she moves seductively around a microphone. Normally that type of thing sends my blood rushing, but tonight, the only thing doing it for me is the thought of a certain brunette in a white bikini.

What are the women up to? If we have this type of entertainment, I don't doubt they do too. There's probably some greasy Croat sliding his oily skin against Emma right now, all in the name of a bit of fun. Though I have no claim on her at all, the thought sickens me.

Abby's father, Noel, sits to my right, Callum's brother, Brian, to my left. I can't concentrate on the game. Brian's acing it, like he does everything in life, by all accounts.

Noel lights a cigar, and I try not to cough in his face. I don't smoke. I don't often drink, though sometimes I do to help me forget. I've never been able to train and drink, it's always been one or the other. Training's going well, so I know from experience it would only take a few of those small tumblers, and I'd be three sheets to the wind. I don't plan on wasting tonight's sleepover with Emma hugging the toilet bowl.

'What's her name, son?' Noel leans towards me inconspicuously.

I sit back a fraction and look at him, wondering if he's taking the piss. He wasn't at the pool earlier.

'Whose name?' I bluff.

'Her name is Emma,' Brian answers for me with a knowing smirk.

Noel sits forward and pushes more chips forward. 'What's the serious face for? Are you in the dog house or something, son?' He takes a long deep drag of the cigar, exhaling a cloud of smoke into my face. 'I will be, by the way, if Cathy Queenan catches me with this cigar.' He glances down at the chunky brown guilty pleasure between his index finger and thumb with a deep-rooted sense of appreciation. 'You're never too old for a bollocking. Thirty years married last year. I'd have done less time for murder.'

I can't help but snigger. Noel doesn't say much, but I know Callum has a lot of respect for him.

'I think you have to be in the main house, to be thrown out to the dog house. I'm currently barking at the front gate.' I wink at him. 'But I think I'm pretty close to being thrown a bone, if you know what I mean.'

Noel slaps the table and guffaws. 'Well, good luck with that, son.'

'You were let in the front gate before if I remember rightly,' Brian muses, as he watches the rolling dice with expectant eyes.

'Ahh, but did he get the bone?' Nathan raises his eyebrows across the table. I deliberately ignore his question. That is between Emma and me.

'*If* I get back in again, I'm going to lock that fucking gate and throw away the key.' I have no intention of fucking this up a second time. If only I can earn her trust enough to get the chance to prove it to her. She's confident, assertive, and strong-minded. Far from intimidating me, she intrigues me. How could a smart woman like her be interested in me; the team joker, the class clown? My current favourite trick is hiding my own misery behind other people's laughter. It's a defence mechanism. If they're laughing, they might not notice the permanent cloud that hovers over me.

A text pings through on my phone. It's Amy, my younger sister.

Found a vehicle for Matt. Automatic. From Mobility Ireland. Everything is going to plan x

My recent elation comes crashing down as reality slaps me around the face. It's good news, great, in fact. Between the house and the car, Matt's return is going to plan. It's just a shame that the concept of him returning was not part of *his* plan.

That familiar feeling of self-loathing creeps in, curling its multiple tentacles around my heart. My brother may never walk again, and it's my fault. Yet here I am, swanning around, pretending I'm something I'm not. For a couple of hours there, I allowed the change of scenery, sunshine and cocktails to go to my head.

Emma might be what I need, but I'm definitely not what she needs. She deserves so much better than a fuck up like me. I shouldn't have kissed her like that. If she knew what I'd done, she wouldn't come anywhere near me. I have no right to pursue her. Just like I didn't last September.

I grip my temples between my fingers and try to fight the feeling of despair for now. I have no time to confront my demons at this precise moment. Not here, not now. I repeat the mantra silently in my head until I feel stronger. But they'll catch up with me shortly. They always do.

Only two things give me the temporary reprieve from the monstrous memories that lurk in my mind: exercise or alcohol. Seeing as I can't exactly head for the treadmill, I submit to the inevitable other, taking a glass from the passing server and downing the whisky in one go. I replace the glass and take another one immediately, all thoughts of happiness with Emma shoved aside again. A man like me doesn't deserve it.

CHAPTER SIXTEEN

EMMA

'The boys aren't the only ones that have some fun planned.' Alicia takes her niece from Abby and hands her over to Mrs Queenan, who arrives at the poolside with her rollers twisted in her hair already.

'Trying them out before the big day,' she explains to Alicia, patting her head.

'She's due a feed in about an hour,' Abby instructs her mother, accepting her fate.

I have no idea what Alicia has planned, but I'm ninety-nine per cent sure I'm not dressed suitably for it.

'Shall we go and get ready?'

'You are ready. Apart from some accessories, of course.' Alicia produces ten rose gold hen party sashes from her beach bag and a packet of penis-shaped straws. She hands the merchandise out. Karen and Fran eye each other with disgust, but put them on as we are told.

'Who are the other ones for? We seem to have too many,' Abby says.

'Nadine and Melissa, of course. And your school friends from Carrick. They'll be here any minute.'

'I'm not going to some teenybopper foam party in a bikini, Alicia,' Abby says, doubtfully looking down at her tiny swimwear.

'No, you're not. Have a little faith, sis. I know what you like.'

The waiter from earlier approaches us, his name tag says Jacov. 'More drinks, ladies?' He offers a knowing wink.

'No, thank you, it looks like we are leaving.' I pull myself up from the poolside and walk back to my sunlounger.

'You're not going anywhere,' he says in a low voice, tapping the side of his nose conspicuously. He points to a karaoke machine only partially visible from behind the wooden drinks hut. 'Warm up those vocal chords, Irish.'

I seem to have acquired a new nickname. I kind of like it.

I'm not actually a bad singer. Holly and I used to do a great Tina Turner impression, but I hate doing it. Everyone thinks I love the limelight. I don't. I'm semi-clothed, only partially concealed, and mentally freaking out after Eddie's kiss. I'm a mess. I can't sing in front of everyone too. What if they see how Eddie shook my world? What if I can't hide my thoughts? Ultimately, what if I let him in, and the second we get home he goes back to her?

'Better bring us another couple of jugs then, I suppose.' At least I don't have to get up and put my warpaint on.

Today has been lovely, not having to pose as the face of my very own beauty empire. In Dublin, I always feel like I have to demonstrate flawless skin and immaculate hair and nails as an advertisement for my business. Maintaining a certain image all the time is exhausting. Even Karen and Kerry mistake my insecurity for vanity. I prefer it that way. Paul apparently saw through it though, saw me for what I am.

'I make you something special. So you don't miss your boyfriend too much.' Jacov winks at me.

'He's not my boyfriend!'

'You sign the same room number. You eat the same sandwich. He is your boyfriend, no?'

'No, no, no, you misunderstand.' I shake my head vigorously, though unsure why I'm explaining myself to a middle-aged Croatian waiter.

'You kiss him like he is the love of your life.' Jacov chuckles and shrugs. 'My mistake.' He saunters off to make the drinks. Huh. He might well have been the love of my life if he hadn't just taken off the next day, without so much as a glance back over his shoulder. I really need to get over that, but it's easier said than done.

Mrs Queenan is showing absolutely no sign of making shapes with the baby. In fact she clicks her fingers at Jacov and orders three bottles of champagne.

'Where's the pram?' I hear her ask Abby. It looks like baby Casey is going to be attending her first hen night.

Within the hour, we are joined by six more women, and the free-flowing drink has lubricated everyone's joints. The girls dance barefoot around palm trees in front of the pool. I sit back, taking it all in from the chair that Eddie vacated a short while earlier, still unable to quite get in the swing of things.

I'm overanalysing Eddie's kiss, replaying it, questioning its depth, its meaning. No wonder I can't keep a man. I'm already crazily wondering where this is going to lead, apart from the obvious place, of course.

Karen is belting out Madonna's 'Like a Prayer' like her life depends on it. A few hotel guests hover nearby, watching the show. A lifeguard perches high up at his station, watching as the women get more and more out of hand, and more likely to need rescuing at some point. Alicia must have paid dearly

for this privilege tonight, or someone did. The pool technically closes at 8 p.m. and the ropes have been put up, penning
us in.

'You're up next, Emma,' Kerry squeals at me.

'No way, you go first. Age before beauty.' I wink at her,
and she sticks her tongue out at me but sways towards the
karaoke machine anyway. A couple of minutes later, I hear the
first few bars of Hot Chocolate's 'You Sexy Thing', and I
know our audience are in for a treat. This is Kerry's party
piece from college; I only hope she doesn't injure herself with
the exotic dance moves that accompany it.

'You okay?' Abby materialises from nowhere and sits next
to me.

'Grand, thanks. Are you?' It's her hen night. She should be
necking shots and shaking her limbs like the rest of them.

She takes one of my hands and squeezes it meaningfully.
'Give him a chance, Em.'

'I did. And look what happened the last time. It's your
hen, let's not talk about it tonight.' I drain the remainder of
my drink.

'I want to talk about it,' Abby says. It's the shrink in her. I
recognise the change in her tone, she's switched to her radio
voice again.

'Look, I tried not to let it show before, but that man
knocked the wind out of my sails the last time. And I could
have sworn it was mutual. Otherwise, I never would have...
Well, you know my three-date rule.' I wring my wrists as I
remember.

'Callum told me last night what happened. Look, it's none
of my business and it's definitely not my place to tell, but
Eddie has had a really rough time of it since that weekend.'
Abby stares at Kerry, wrapping her leg seductively around the
microphone pole before dropping to the floor and up again.

Her bikini top is dangerously off-kilter. If she's not careful, she could end up losing it.

'It can't have been that bad when he shacked up with Maria.'

'She was a distraction.'

'Well, why couldn't I have been that distraction? It just seems a bit of a coincidence that the very weekend he promises me the earth, moon and stars, he swans off to the States, never to be seen again, until now, of course. Whatever predicament he got into...it didn't stop him from dating another woman.'

Abby nods thoughtfully before answering in a low tone. 'You might think this is my agony aunt psychobabble spiel talking, but hear me out. When things don't work out the way we hope, a lot of us have a tendency to turn it around on ourselves, take it personally. Overanalyse the situation. And in some instances, this can be a good thing, because it's how we learn and grow and adapt our ways. It was unfortunate that you broke your three-date rule for Eddie, and then it didn't work out. No wonder you feel used. But it wasn't something you did or didn't do. It was the circumstances. You should talk to him about it, maybe he'll explain it himself. I'm pretty sure he's all yours...if you want him. He thinks you deserve better than him, according to Callum.'

What an odd remark to make. How could I deserve better than him? He's the one who is a super-hot sports star, not to mention hilariously funny and drop-dead gorgeous to go alongside it. Something doesn't add up. What on earth happened to him, to shake his confidence so much when he left me that night? I pull a beach towel around myself, unable to fully shake the shiver that runs through my spine.

CHAPTER SEVENTEEN

EDDIE

Staggering the length of the corridor, my fingers grip the wall for support, my legs rock unsteadily beneath me. My skull is splitting in two, and the effects of the alcohol haven't even worn off yet.

My keycard isn't working. I push it into the slot over and over again and it flashes red.

'Stupid fucking door.' I bang it with my fist, aware that I'm not actually angry with the door. I'm angry with myself. Angry for drinking too much, angry for kissing Emma, angry for my past.

The door flies open abruptly and a lanky guy wearing nothing but a pair of boxers and a frown, glares at me. 'What the fuck, man? It's two o'clock in the morning.' His accent is American. Tattooed arms cross defensively over his chest.

'Where's Emma?' Oh fuck, he must be the stripper. Fucking hell, I never should have left her, and I'm not just talking about today.

A woman appears beside him in a white vest and a pair of

greying knickers. 'Let him in, he's kind of cute.' Her accent mimics his, as she rubs a hand over his tattooed arms.

In the open doorway, clothes are strewn untidily around the room, clothes that don't look like mine or Emma's. 'Is this 425? I think I might be in the wrong place.'

'This is 325. I think you're on the wrong floor, but by all means, come in.' The woman opens the door wider, eyeing me from head to toe like I'm the last cream cake in the baker's shop.

'Ah.' I take a step backwards. 'I'm sorry.' I hastily retrace my steps along the corridor, as 'Is that an Irish accent?' echoes after me.

My little encounter sobers me up marginally, at least. In the lift, I press the correct button and eventually find my way to the right room. The keycard works first time. The room is in darkness, but I hear Emma's soft, even breathing from the bed. I reach the couch and remove my shirt and shorts. She flicks the bedside light on with a loud click.

'Ah, I almost missed the show.' A tinkling laugh falls from her lips. She's wearing my rugby jersey again. I'd made my mind up to stop flirting with her, to pull back. Now she's ten feet away from me, with one long bare leg wrapped around the outside of the duvet in that tantalising pose again, I'm reminded of all the reasons that I don't want to.

'Did the strippers not provide enough entertainment?' A stab of shame passes through me, as I realise I immediately thought the worst of her when I'd banged on the wrong door. She deserves way more credit than that.

'Clearly, your night was way more exciting than ours. The only man in the vicinity was Jacov – thank god he does a good Sex On The Beach.' She sits up and curls her legs up into a crossed position underneath her. I'm aware that I'm staring at her, but I can't tear myself away. She arches two perfect eyebrows into an upwards curve, it's a challenge, possibly even an invitation. I stand in limbo, unsure what to do. My balls scream at me to pounce on her, but my brain still warns me that she deserves so much more than what I have to offer.

My split second hesitation speaks volumes to her. She slides her legs back underneath the linen and swiftly leans towards the lamp, clicking it off.

'Don't.' It's out of my mouth before I can overthink it.

'Why? Are you afraid of the dark?'

'No.' I deliberate for a few more seconds before deciding it's time to come clean. The weight of my shame is heavy on my heart. I have to confess.

'I'm afraid that if I don't tell you tonight, what happened last year, I might never tell you.' I swallow hard as she switches the lamp back on. Curious eyes stare intensely into mine. I have her undivided attention.

She pats the edge of the bed and motions for me to sit.

'You really didn't hear?'

'No. I simply assumed I'd given you what you wanted, and that was the end of it.' Her fingers twist around her thick glossy hair.

'I'm so sorry, Emma. You deserve so much better.' I take a deep breath and exhale slowly, searching my mind for the right words. What happened was bad enough, but I feel even worse knowing I hurt her in the crossfire.

'The day after that night, I was flying out to the States to see my brother Matthew and his family. They've been living in Washington for three years.'

She nods in encouragement, as though she remembers. We'd joked about me heading straight to the airport from hers; neither of us wanted to accept the night was over, but I had no clean clothes, and not even a bag packed.

'I was so hungover on the flight.' Regret creeps into my stomach. If only I could take it back. Undo it. Drink less. Go home earlier. A memory of us sipping from the same beer bottle, then tasting the same beer from each other's lips presents itself at the forefront of my mind.

She chews her lip, her hair practically knotted around her fingers now.

'I was hungover but excited, you know?' Both about going on holiday and the fact that I'd met someone that I actually clicked with so instantly.

She listens intently, without interruption.

'When I landed, Matthew was waiting for me in arrivals. He brought me outside, to see his latest purchase, a Mustang, no less.'

Emma nods, encouraging me to continue.

'We had an accident...' I can't bring myself to say the actual words, the specific ones that I know I have to tell her.

'It left him in a wheelchair.'

What I should have said is 'I put him in a wheelchair' – but I don't. I can't even say them out loud to myself. How can I say them to her? She deserves the truth, but I can't say it. It was an accident, but that doesn't change the end result. Before I can summon the courage, she closes the distance between us, placing her arms around my neck. Her hot body presses against mine, a welcoming comfort. I squeeze my eyes tight to stop any embarrassing leakage. Grown men crying is not a good look.

I need her to hear the worst of it. The truth of it. That way, if anything happens between us, she won't be horrified later on. 'He'll probably never walk again, never play rugby with his kids. He'll never walk his daughter down the aisle.'

'It was an accident, Eddie. You're bound to feel guilty it was you he'd come to pick up.' She rubs her hand repeatedly over my spine, light soothing strokes, as sorrow and shame eat into my every organ.

'How is Matthew now?'

'Adapting well. Better than I would have done. I don't

know how he stays so positive, to be honest. He had a dark few months, but counselling seemed to help. His wife Nicky is an absolute angel. The kids are a handful, but they adore him. He tells me he might not be able to walk, but he has more than most.'

I need to tell her the truth of it; she deserves to know what she's letting herself in for, but then I risk losing her, just as I'm beginning to get her back. Pins and needles prickle in my outstretched arms, but I don't want to let her go, revelling in the reassurance of her touch.

'My sisters Keira and Amy have been so supportive. Amy's a physiotherapist. She's adamant she will be able to help him if he comes home. The guilt's eating me alive. You know the worst of it? Matthew is the one trying to comfort me. I should be comforting him. It's all so fucked up.'

Tell her, tell her, tell her, tell her, my brain urges, but my mouth refuses to move. What if she's repulsed by me?

She sighs and pulls me down next to her on the bed, pulling my head on her chest in an almost maternal gesture. 'It must have been so traumatic for you, and all the worry for your brother's recovery. You're bound to feel responsible.' She runs her fingers through my hair, and I close my eyes, sinking into the comfort of an embrace that I'm positive I don't deserve. The soothing rhythm of her heart sends me into a deep dreamless sleep.

———

Blinking twice, I take a second to assess where I am. The dull ache in my skull reminds me I drank one too many Jameson's last night. I lie still, enjoying the sensation of Emma's hot body moulded around me, frightened to move, to end this rare tranquil moment. I don't think I've known peace like it, certainly not since the accident.

A few minutes pass blissfully before Emma very gently disentangles herself from me and slips out of bed into the bathroom. I squeeze my eyes tight shut, not wishing to embarrass her at the lack of privacy this place forces on us. Better that she thinks I'm still asleep. The toilet flushes, and the sound of running water trickles through the room. She scrubs her teeth ridiculously hard with that electric toothbrush.

The soles of her feet gently pad against the tiles towards the coffee machine, followed by the low hissing of heating water. Disappointment seeps in as I realise she's not getting back into bed with me. Though, what did I expect? The fact she'd let me share the bed at all was a wonder. The cuddles were a doubly unexpected bonus.

There's a ripping sound, followed by intense stirring, and the light pitter-pattering of feet approaching again.

'Wakey wakey, sleeping beauty.' She perches on the bed next to me and places two sparkling white cups and two headache tablets down on the bedside locker. The woman is an angel.

'Well, this is all very intimate.' I open my eyes with a smile.

'Don't tell me you've been awake the whole time?' She gasps, widening pupils considering what I might have seen.

'The coffee machine woke me,' I lie to prevent her embarrassment. 'But I had the most amazing dream that I shared this bed with the sexiest brunette I've ever laid eyes on. And she gave me the best hug of my life.' I sit up and rest my back against the headboard. Reaching for the scalding coffee, I pop the tablets in my mouth.

'Well, I had a dream that the man I spent the back end of last year wondering about, opened up to me about why he didn't call.' She bites her lower lip tensely. I can only assume she's wondering if this is a topic I'd rather avoid in the light of day.

'I should have told you about Matthew. I'm sorry.'

I still haven't been entirely honest. I'm torn in two; half of me wants to tell her everything. The other half insists she doesn't need to know. She'll never be able to see past what I've done and I've managed to provide a valid enough reason for not calling.

The coward inside wins, and my lips remain firmly pressed together.

'No, don't apologise. I could have called you. I'm sorry. It was pig-headed pride on my part.' She looks down at her perfectly painted cherry-coloured toenails.

Jesus, the last thing I need is for her to feel bad now. I try to lighten the tone in my usual manner.

'I've often wondered what might have happened between us, you know, if I'd just come back from that holiday as planned.' I flash her my biggest brightest smile to plaster over the cracks in my story.

'Me too. Then I met Paul. Huh.' She reaches for her own mug, cradling it between both hands.

'And I met Maria.'

'Well, I'm glad they're not here anyway.'

If I'd have thought for a second she'd still want me, the second I landed back in the country after that awful trip, I'd have rushed straight back to her arms.

'That makes two of us.'

Her full lips curl upwards into a smile. The natural look really suits her. She doesn't need the make-up she wears. It's like she can read my mind; she puts a hand up to her face, as if to hide from me.

'You are beautiful, Emma, the natural look suits you.'

She raises her eyebrows, a look of disbelief in her emerald eyes.

'You have to be joking? I spend my life trying to cover these awful patches on my face. I've even invested in a whole new business in an attempt to find a cure. If you hadn't laid yourself so bare to me last night, I would already be in the bathroom trying to cover them up. But when I put it in perspective against your worries, I sound ridiculous, shallow even.'

'You're a good woman, Emma. You know you have a reputation for being a ball-breaker, right?'

A tinkling laugh pierces the air, and she shrugs.

'Can I ask you something?' I take her free hand with mine, tracing the lines of her palm with my thumb. My heart hammers spiritedly in my chest. She might shoot me down, but if I don't ask, I'll always wonder.

'That depends what it is.' She straightens herself so as not to spill hot coffee all over her legs.

'Now you know why I didn't call, can I take you out sometime? Properly, I mean. I wasn't bullshitting you at the time. I swear we really had something.'

Her silence is deafening as she reverts back to chewing her bottom lip again. I close the remaining distance between us, then brush my thumb over her cheek. Her face tilts towards mine, but she's yet to meet my gaze. Perhaps she's disgusted with me after all? Does she suspect?

'After Paul, I promised myself a break from dating. I'm sick of wasting my time with the wrong men.' Her knee bounces with a nervous kind of energy.

'What if I promise not to waste your time?' I cup her chin in my hand and raise her face the final inch to look at mine.

'Don't make any promises you won't be able to keep.' Her voice is barely more than a whisper. She yanks her head away and jumps to her feet in a cat-like spring.

But it wasn't a no...

CHAPTER EIGHTEEN

EMMA

Eddie exposed a deeper layer of himself last night. The harrowing look in his haunted eyes penetrated my soul. With that slight rawness to his character, stripped from all his usual humour, he's never been more attractive to me. I see flickers of myself in him, outwardly cocky, but secretly unsure, or insecure. Perhaps we have more in common than we originally realised. Though I can't help feeling he's holding something back from me, but I'm probably being paranoid after everything. I'm finding it hard to believe it's really over with Maria, that he's here and single, looking to give it another go. It almost seems too good to be true.

'Room number, please,' the waitresses asks as we are led to a breakfast table next to open French doors.

'Four-two-five,' Eddie answers. This is so weird – like we are a couple, but not. Butterflies in my stomach multiply as I realise it's an idea I could get used to.

'Tea or coffee?' the waitress asks as she places my napkin on my lap.

'Coffee,' we say in unison, sharing a small smile.

'So does this count as our first date then?' Eddie says with a shy grin, leaning forward and taking my hand across the table. His hand strokes the back of mine. I consider pulling away, but I like the sensation too much.

'I suppose we could call it that...'

'So what are we doing today?'

He is very presumptuous this morning. Though if breakfast was our first date, lunch could be our second...then by the time we have dinner tonight, we'll have ticked the three-date rule. I might not have to insist he sleeps on the couch again. The thought sends a shooting pang of longing through me.

I push back my filthy thoughts for now. 'Some exploring?'

'What about one of those boat tours round the smaller islands?' he suggests.

'Great idea. We better make the most of the day because tomorrow we could be roped into anything in preparation for the wedding of the year.'

'You think? Abby strikes me as the kind of person who has everything under control.'

'Yeah, but who knows what Mrs Queenan might throw into the works.'

Marcus, Ollie and the other teammate, Nathan, walk into the dining room. Marcus's balding head is gleaming with sweat already, but it's not nearly as bright as his goofy grin when he spots Eddie holding my hand for all to see.

'Well, well, what do we have here? I see you two picked up where you left off yesterday.' Marcus approaches and slaps Eddie on the back. Turning to me he points at Nathan and says, 'No wonder you had no interest in Barbie over there; you had your sights set on Ken all along.'

A text lights up my phone on the table in front of me. I'd never normally have it out on the table, especially not if this *is* a first date, but now it's Monday, I'm desperate for an update from Sarah regarding the Balbriggan property. I'd temporarily forgotten about it last night with Eddie's revelation.

'Everything okay?' Eddie nods at the phone.

'Yes. I'm waiting on an update on my latest business venture.'

'You're some woman, you know that? Running a beauty empire, how many salons do you have now?'

'Four. And I'm about to acquire a fifth premises; it's going to be a luxury spa.' I recognise the excitement in my own voice as I imagine the launch party.

'Sounds intriguing. Tell me more.' Eddie tucks into the plateful of food that the waitress placed in front of him.

'I don't want to jinx it, but you will be the first to know when I sign the contract; hell, if you play your cards right, I might even invite you to my big swish opening.'

'Who knows...I might even come.' A devilish look takes over his face, and I get the impression he's not merely talking about the launch.

CHAPTER NINETEEN

EDDIE

While Emma gathers a few belongings from the room, I head to reception to book a boat excursion. We're in luck. There's a boat leaving in less than an hour, exploring three islands, with a BBQ to finish. I ring Emma to tell her to hurry.

'Hello?'

'There's a boat leaving in an hour. If we hurry, we'll make it.'

Silence from the other end of the phone. 'Emma?'

'You kept my number.' Her breathy tone sounds kind of stunned.

'Of course I did. I'm just a fool I didn't dial it earlier. Now hurry up, we have an awesome day ahead. Can you grab me a baseball cap out of my bag?'

'Sure. See you in five.'

Elation skyrockets within at the natural level of comfort we have achieved so quickly. Jees, in the few months I dated Maria, I never even told her my brother is in a wheelchair.

You still haven't told Emma the truth, the demon whispers, but I swat him away, unwilling to risk our fresh start.

————

Twelve of us wait to board the boat; six couples. Two of the couples are in their fifties and seem to be related. They sport identical white ankle socks, brown leather sandals and matching British accents. A couple in their late twenties look like they could be on honeymoon; gazing adoringly at each other, twisting bright shining rings on their wedding fingers and exchanging regular meaningful squeezes.

The fourth couple are two men, one decidedly older than the other, but the way they kiss leaves little to the imagination. The last couple, other than us, are definitely Irish. The fair skin and red hair would give them away if the Ireland rugby jersey didn't. I've seen them before. I'm pretty certain they're staying in the same hotel as us. The guy repeatedly glances over at us, and I'm fairly sure he's contemplating approaching for an autograph. I'm used to it, but the last thing I need is to get saddled with some rugby fanatic when I'm hoping to rekindle some romance with Emma.

Varnished wooden planks, skilfully sculpt the boat into a historic looking vessel. Four picnic benches occupy the centre, evenly spaced apart. A single narrow bench runs either side of the boat, for the passengers that prefer to sit close to the water.

Emma takes my hand as she boards the makeshift ramp, her slim manicured fingers anchoring into mine. A swell of protection rises in my chest. I can't believe I did the disappearing act on her. I was so consumed with what was happening across the Atlantic. As if she can read my mind, she squeezes my fingers and smiles back reassuringly at me.

'Where do you want to sit?' I glance around at available spots.

She pulls me towards a bench on the edge of the boat. A ripple of mild surprise passes through me. After discovering her fear of flying and heights, I was inclined to think she'd prefer the table in the centre.

'Thought you had me sussed, didn't you?' Her sensuous lips curl into a smirk.

'I'd be a fool to make that claim.'

'I'm not exactly sporty, but I'm an okay swimmer.' She sits close to me, her bare thigh resting against mine. I chance dropping an arm around her shoulder, and she doesn't brush it away, busy absorbing our surroundings. The captain introduces himself to us as Bob, and his two crewmen are David and Petar. Following a brief demonstration regarding basic housekeeping, the captain starts the engine.

We cruise at a leisurely twenty kilometres an hour. The Elafiti Islands are stunning on the horizon. Petar explains that the three we are scheduled to visit today are Kolocep, Lopud and Sipan. Emma listens attentively, gazing out across the sea, her shoulders relaxed underneath my arm.

First stop is Kolocep, the smallest of the islands. We disembark and are given half an hour of free time to explore, but opt to spend it on the sandy beach. She slips off the shoulders of her dress to sunbathe, and I try not to stare at the taught looking skin of her cleavage.

I brush a stray strand of hair from her face in a deliberate attempt to get close to her. 'So, have you had many serious relationships?'

'Where did that come from?' Surprise infiltrates her darting eyes.

'Just wondering about my competition. Isn't that a kind of first date thing to discuss?' I laugh to hide the true nature of my curiosity.

'Have you?' she retorts.

Touché. With only a foot between us, I notice her chest barely moves, her breath appears almost caught as she awaits my answer.

'No. Maria definitely wasn't serious. It only lasted as long as it did because we lived in different countries.' I pick up a handful of sand and watch as it slowly slips through my fingers.

'I used to wonder what she did differently to me. Then I decided she mustn't have slept with you on the first night. Smart woman.' Emma's lips raise upwards, but she can't fully manage to pass her remark off as a joke.

'That's all it ever really was, to be honest, casual sex. She used to constantly pick fights with me to get my attention, because in all honesty, I couldn't give it to her. I had too much else on my mind. Her demands distracted me from what I should have been dealing with.'

'Are you one hundred per cent sure it's over with her?'

'I swear to you, Emma, it's over this time. No amount of persuasion in the world would send me back to her.' It's the absolute truth and I try my utmost to convey my sincerity to her with my eyes. She glances brightly up at me from under jet black elongated eyelashes. I wonder for a second if they are real, before realising I don't care either way. Throwing a pebble into the sea, I watch as it skips and hops the crystal water five times before sinking completely.

Dusting sand from our legs, we make our way back to the boat, and resume our previous seats for the next part of the excursion; 'the middle island' Lopud. Emma relaxes against me, quietly comfortable, watching and listening until we arrive. Being with her like this feels like the most natural thing in the world.

After another short journey, we disembark once again.

This time we have two hours free time to find some lunch and explore, before regrouping back at the boat at two o'clock for our final part of the tour and the BBQ on the boat.

'Have you got a bikini on under that dress?' I ask her. Today's blue dress isn't nearly as revealing as yesterday's white one.

'Are you being practical or curious?' Emma's eyes alight with mischief. 'Because, contrary to our first encounter, I'm usually not that kind of girl.' Girlish peals of laughter burst from her chest.

'What I probably should have said is, do you want to go for a swim or a walk?'

'Neither.' We stray from the crowd, strolling through paths of lush vegetation and approach a small bike hire hut.

'How's your cycling?' She points to a small shack with bikes to hire.

'I wouldn't have had you pegged for a cyclist.' I eye her long painted nails, which may be pretty, but are less than practical.

'Who said anything about me cycling?' She points to a tandem and laughs.

'Seriously?'

I pay the young local manning the bike hire and follow signs for Sunj Bay. For a tall girl, Emma feels light on the back of the tandem. The two of us laugh as we speed around the winding bendy lanes with the wind in our hair and the sun on our faces.

'We need to get a picture of this,' she calls from behind.

I brake to a gentle stop and pull my phone out of my pocket, delighted she's giving me an excuse to capture this moment.

The screen of my phone shows fifteen missed calls, four voicemails and thirty-two WhatsApp messages. Shit. With all the fun I'd been having I forgot about my responsibilities back at home.

'Everything okay?' Emma calls, when I don't immediately start snapping.

'Yes, I just have to deal with something first, sorry.' I hold the phone up to my ear and listen to my sister's four, increasingly frantic messages.

'Eddie, we've been outbid on the house for Matthew again. How far are you willing to go?'

'Eddie, I know you told me not to mention it to Matthew, but I spoke to him yesterday, and he sounded pretty down about coming home, so I told him we had the house practically sorted. I don't want to have to tell him we lost it. Ring me back, please.'

'Eddie, if we don't do this now we are going to lose this house. Ring me back asap.'

'Where the fuck are you? I thought you were in Croatia, not no man's land. Call me.'

Fuck. Fuck. Fuck. I redial Keira's direct line in her fancy office on Grafton Street, my heart hammering in my ribcage. Sweat pumps from my brow, and it's more to do with my own foolishness than my efforts with the tandem. I shouldn't have taken my eye off the ball. It's Monday, for fuck's sake! I should have been watching the phone until the deal was official.

'Harrington, Harper and Henry.' My sister's secretary answers.

'It's Eddie. Is Keira there?'

'She's just popped out the office for a second. Hang on and I'll have a look for her.' The gentle sounds of Mozart's Symphony No. 40 exit through the receiver, and my knee bounces impatiently, rocking the tandem.

'Easy.' Emma giggles from behind.

'Sorry, there's just a problem with the—'

'Eddie?' Keira calls over the receiver.

'Keira. Sorry. I'm here. How much?' I run my thumb over my stubble as I wait. Money is not a problem. I should have made that clear. Whatever it is, I'll make it work.

'One point five million.' She breathes heavily over the phone.

'Sound. Make it happen, Keira.' Someone wants this almost as badly as me. Well, tough, I will do whatever I have to, to make things easier for Matthew. Losing is not something I can live with.

'That's all I needed to hear. I'll fax the hotel the paperwork as soon as I have it. You okay, little brother?' Concern etches into her maternal tone.

'Sound.' I glance back at Emma, the panic evaporating from my body once again. That was close.

CHAPTER TWENTY

EMMA

While Eddie's distracted, I check my phone and find a message from Sarah containing row upon row of champagne emojis.

We outbid them again. It's currently yours.

I type a quick text back, trying to hide the grin that's threatening to take over my face, while Eddie sounds so serious from the seat in front of me.

Stay on top of it. No last-minute overtakers.

I put my phone back into the satchel that's crossed over my shoulder and look up at Eddie, whose grin is almost as wide as my own.

'Let's find one of those hotels and grab a celebratory drink,' Eddie says.

'Great idea. I'm parched. But what are we celebrating?' I hold my own news close to my chest for now, still wondering who Keira is.

'That was my sister. She's a solicitor. Matthew is moving home next month. I'm buying him a house, as a welcome home present. It's just a few doors down from mine, so I'll be able to help them out and spend loads of time with the kids too. I'm just waiting for the paperwork now.'

'It looks like we both have something to celebrate. I'm hours away from securing my dream location for the spa.' I can't wipe the smile from my face.

'This calls for champagne.' Eddie hops back onto his seat and begins to pedal again. We cycle the length of the beach with the gentle breeze blowing through my hair and the salt on my face.

He stops pedalling as we approach a hotel and twists his head to look at me.

'How about here?'

'It looks fancy. I think I might be underdressed.'

'Emma Harvey, you could never be underdressed.' He winks at me with a knowing smirk, and my stomach somersaults.

A waitress leads us to a white wicker table in the outdoor dining area, overlooking the sandy shore. She drags out the chair for me, opposite Eddie. A blue and white checked table cloth lifts with the light sea breeze as we examine the menus she provided us with. It truly is paradise.

'Are you hungry?' I ask him.

'I'm always hungry.' Eddie rubs his stomach, and his shirt lifts with the motion, revealing a perfect trail of fine dark hair that descends into navy shorts. He skilfully arches a single eyebrow as I stare lustfully at his bare skin.

'See anything you like?' His lips part a fraction, just enough for him to lick them. And I thought I was the flirt.

'Do you?'

Touché. I sit forward, rest one elbow on the table in front of me and squeeze my cleavage together under his nose.

'So, we're back to these games, are we?' He takes a lungful of air and exhales it slowly onto my chest.

'Who will win?' I sit back once again and tilt my head to the side.

'If we play our cards right, I've got a feeling we both might.' His smile extends all the way to his darkening eyes.

'Have you got any sun cream on?' I ask.

'No. And I've no sunlounger to lie face down on either, so it's probably best if we keep our hands to ourselves, for now at least.' A throaty laugh travels across the table.

As Eddie orders a bottle of champagne, I reach into my handbag and pull out a miniature of one of my brand-new products, a light, silky moisturiser with an SPF of 50. I toss it across the table, and he picks it up, squinting at the turquoise label.

'Serapy? What is this stuff? I've never heard of it.'

'Ah, not yet. But you will soon. Can you keep a secret?' I'm dying to tell him, especially now I'm only hours away from closing the deal, and the champagne is en route.

He examines the bottle again and does the Eddie single eyebrow raise again, the one I've come to love over the past two days. Did I just say love? I meant like immensely. Obviously.

'It's mine. I made it. Well, designed, developed and branded. It's part of my brand-new skincare range I'm going to launch alongside the spa.'

'Wow. That's fantastic, Emma. Congratulations.' He inspects the back of the silver bottle. '*Lovingly made by Emma Harvey.*' He lets out a low whistle. 'Your family must be so proud of you.'

I push my sunglasses up on to my nose to hide the fact that he's accidentally stumbled upon my secret motivation.

'Not yet, to be honest. If my mother has a soft centre, I'm yet to find it, but I plan on being so successful that even she can't ignore it.'

'Seriously? Emma, this is such an amazing achievement.

I'm so fucking proud of you.' He pushes his chair back, crouches next to me and throws his arms around my waist in a hug that has his head resting on my chest.

The waitress arrives with the champagne at the same time, and patrons on the neighbouring tables begin to clap. Table by table, the clapping escalates, and Eddie and I skilfully exchange an entire conversation without saying a word. If I wasn't so embarrassed, I might actually be delighted that we've joined the ranks of the seriously talented, silently united couples as we manage an entire conversation with only our eyes.

Are they clapping at us?

Do they think...?

Well, you are crouching down beside me...

Holy fuck...

Eddie stands and returns to his seat, nodding awkwardly at everyone surrounding us and accepts a glass of the bubbling flute offered. Neither of us confirm nor deny the public misunderstanding. Eventually, the clapping dies down, and people return to their drinks.

I raise my slim crystal flute and clink it against Eddie's. I can't believe people thought he was actually proposing to me.

'That was *so* embarrassing.' And more so because it's an idea I'd potentially love, way down the line, of course.

'Who knows? It could be a premonition...' Eddie raises his glass again.

'Hah. I wouldn't have you down as the marriage type.' Not for the first time this holiday, I'm unbelievably grateful my sunglasses mask half my face. I'm testing the water. I know I am.

'You'd be surprised.' He takes a sip of his drink and places it down on the table. 'My family are always giving me shit about it. You aren't the first person to call me the baby whisperer.'

My mind strays back to yesterday, by the pool. The way he was so capable with Abby's baby; so confident, so loving, so tender. My heart leaps wildly in my chest. Could he be serious? All of the men I've previously encountered have run at the first hint that I wanted children. Sharing a bottle of champagne in sunny Dubrovnik with Ireland's rugby hooker, who just so happens to want to settle down and have a family one day seems almost too good to be true. Dare I hope that I may have kissed the final frog, even if it is for the second time?

He interrupts my thoughts, bringing me back to the moment. 'So, if breakfast did happen to count as our first official date, does lunch count as our second?'

'Ha! I have to wonder why you are so desperate to put a label on them? By any chance, did any little birdies tell you about my three-date rule?' I reposition my sunglasses on my nose and stare intently at him for any tell-tale clues.

'No, but it sounds pretty intriguing.' He picks up a king prawn from the seafood platter the waitress subtly placed between us and breaks it in two.

'Well, it kind of speaks for itself.'

'I see.' He runs a thumb over his chin in that thoughtful fashion that he does so often. 'And do you ever break that rule, or is it more of a rough guideline?' His lip lifts into a crooked smile.

'I only ever broke it once.' I push my glasses up on top of my head, so I can meet his eye.

Within a millisecond, his face falls. 'Oh, Emma, I'm so sorry.' He takes my hand across the table, even though we are both covered in seafood.

'It's fine. It wasn't, but it is now I know.' I give his hands a gentle squeeze.

'You must have thought I was a total twat. Actually, I am a total twat.'

'I have this superpower ability to attract them.' I wink at him to show I'm joking, about him at least, not the others.

'Worse than me? You managed to wangle out of the question earlier; don't think I didn't notice how you completely turned it around on me.' He raises an eyebrow in question.

'Me? Never.' He's busted me. If I want this to go anywhere, I need to start on a foundation of honesty. No point pretending to be someone I'm not, because so far, pretending has got me absolutely nowhere.

'I've had them all. The Time Waster, The Womaniser, The Mammy's Boy, The Bad Boy, The Alcoholic, The Man Child and lastly, Paul; The Workaholic.' My hands raise up in a 'this is me' pose, and I smile, hoping he doesn't pity me. Truly, I couldn't give a shit about any of them, well, apart from the one sitting opposite me right this second.

'And which category did I fall under?' Eddie sits forward now with two elbows on the table, his attention entirely focused on me.

'Ha. I'm not sure if I should even tell you what I called you.' A small unladylike snort escapes my grinning lips.

'Well, now I'm dying to know. Come on, don't hold back; I deserve it.' His eyes are alight with curiosity, his tone jovial. There are apparently no hard feelings between us.

'You were The One That Got Away,' I confess with a shrug.

'Wow. That's deep. At least that is something I can rectify, I hope?' He takes both my hands again, leans forward over the table and plants the gentlest brush of a kiss on my lips, sending tremors through me.

'You already did.' I take a deep breath, inhaling his familiar scent before he pulls back.

'By the way, I'm taking you out tonight. And technically, it will be our third date.' He winks knowingly at me, and I throw my napkin across the table at him and laugh.

His hair falls over his left eye as his attention returns to the fresh lobster. He brushes it away with a huge, solid hand. A hand that I want to brush over me. I'm in serious danger of falling hard for The One That Got Away. I was half in love with him after the first night. Now I know his story, his truth, and with Maria truly out of the picture, Eddie has developed a new, increasingly appealing allure.

The waitress clears our plates away, and he asks for the bill. We ought to be getting back. I remove my phone from my bag to check the time. The message from Sarah lighting up my screen winds me.

Outbid – again. Whoever it is, means business. 1.7 million. I'm so sorry.

Shit. My stomach somersaults, a nervous apprehension tingles through my spine. Who the hell could be so persistent with their counter bids? For a split second, I consider the prospect that I might actually fail to secure this property. It doesn't even bear thinking about.

I've poured blood, sweat and tears into this new venture. The location is paramount to its success. Properties like this one do not come up often. I took a chance, marketing my new range with images of the sea to enhance the appeal of a locally sourced natural skin ingredient: seaweed. If I don't get it over the line now, the hundreds of thousands that I've wasted in product testing will be wasted. Not to mention the multiple jobs depending on this.

Failing at love is one thing. Failing at business is not an option.

CHAPTER TWENTY-ONE

EDDIE

'I need to make a phone call. Sorry.' Emma excuses herself and heads towards the beach with her phone pressed firmly to her ear.

'Is everything okay?' I ask the second she returns.

'It will be. Sometimes you have to play dirty when it comes to getting things you want. Especially in business.' She shrugs and hops on to the back saddle.

We return the bike to the owner. Bob, David and Petar welcome us back onto the boat. Emma checks her phone once more before throwing it back into her bag and sighing deeply.

'Thank you for lunch, by the way. I didn't mean to just rush off.'

'No problem. Shall I book somewhere in the old town for dinner tonight?'

She bites her lower lip to halt the grin erupting on her face. 'I thought we're having a BBQ on the boat? Remember? We'll go out for cocktails with the others instead. We really should spend some time with our friends, you know. I've barely seen the girls since we got here.'

She doesn't sound too upset about it, but she's right. The rugby team's WhatsApp group is hopping. Marcus has photoshopped a picture of my face onto a missing ad on a milk bottle and shared it. Fucker. Was it only last night that we were in the makeshift casino? It feels like a lifetime ago.

David struts around the boat, offering everyone fruity orange cocktails, Tequila Sunrises he calls them. Only this morning, I swore I was never drinking again, yet here I am. Coach will kill me if I fuck up this weekend's match.

Petar begins his talk on our final destination, Sipan, which we can see looming on the horizon. Emma has resumed her position, her shoulders tucked firmly underneath my arm, like they were made to fit there. I draw circles on her exposed shoulder blades and watch as goosebumps ripple her skin.

'If I tip David, does that count as buying you a cocktail? We can tick off date three as done?'

She throws her head back in amusement. 'Someone's keen.' Her grin exposes ivory, symmetrical teeth.

'Three dates, you said?' My question earns me a swift dig in the ribs. For a split second, I wonder what will happen when we get home, back to Dublin. Will we continue our easy banter? Or is she one of these super busy career women that's more devoted to her business than any lover?

Wow. Lover? Jesus, one fabulous night almost a year ago hardly still counts as a lover. I'm getting ahead of myself here, though a man can hope, right?

The red-haired guy and his partner eventually approach, each holding one of David's cocktails.

'Hi.' I scoot up along the bench to make room for them.

'It's fabulous, isn't it?' Emma says to the woman, gesturing to the landscape.

'It sure is. We're a long way from home.' The woman's

accent projects a distinct musical lilt associated with Donegal.

'Are you..?' The guy tilts his head curiously at me. I can tell it's been killing him all day.

'Eddie Harrington. Pleased to meet you. This is Emma, my girlfriend.' Okay, that's a stretch, but I'm working on it. I reluctantly remove my arm from around Emma's bare shoulders and shake hands with my fellow countryman.

'I'm Donal, this is my girlfriend, Denise. It's so good to meet you, man, I'm a massive fan.' He glances down at his rugby shirt and laughs.

Emma leans closer into my chest. She definitely didn't object to the girlfriend remark.

'Big game this weekend for ye,' Donal reminds me.

'Yeah. Hopefully, we'll do it. Never can be too confident. The odds might not be in our favour, especially after the week away from training.' I force the frown from my face as I think about it.

Marcus is in the doghouse as the video of his poolside streak yesterday made this morning's Irish gossip columns. Ava Armstrong is a notoriously vicious celebrity journalist, turned chat show host. She thrives on ripping celebrity relationships apart, causing trouble where there is none, and calling it news. Her morning television broadcast a clip of Marcus's streak, followed immediately by a video of his wife Shelly battling to strap their daughters into the aforementioned Audi in the lashing rain. I only caught a glimpse of it, but her underlying message was clear; it's a man's world.

'What game?' Emma whispers as our two new companions sit next to us.

I lean in towards her, deliberately brushing my lips over her earlobes. 'Leinster versus Munster. Sunday. Will you come?'

Illuminated eyes twinkle up at me. 'Do you want me to?'

'Of course.'

Eventually, we arrive at Sipan, and Bob anchors the boat. Our new friends look disappointed as we wave goodbye, but I'm desperate to get Emma back to myself. We agree to meet back before six.

'Let's find a nice hotel.' She reaches out for my hand as she steps off the boat, less cautiously than the first two times.

'Are you serious?' I knew she was forward, but I hadn't taken the cocktail as our third date literally.

Laughter bursts from Emma's well-endowed chest, and for a second, I'm really not sure what to make of her.

'For a drink. Preferably one with sunloungers, so I can work on my tan,' she says as my rapidly pumping pulse slows again.

'Oh.'

'Something else on the brain?' She arches into me, so her face is millimetres from mine, her body pressing intimately against mine. I'm aware of her every curve. I'm also aware that we are in public. And at least one person on this island is dying to get a photo of me. If one like this hit the headlines, Maria would likely hire an assassin to obliterate me. Technically it's only been two days since we split. Two beautiful Emma-filled days. Two of the best days of my life.

The alcohol's made me reckless. I take my chances with the assassin, pulling Emma into me, holding her firmly against me. Our bodies press tightly together as I bend my head down to access her full, parted lips. Our mouths meet with a ferocity I couldn't have predicted. Though it's not our first kiss, something's changed. A deepened level of want, following our recent unexpected bonding. There's a familiarity to the way that her tongue searches for mine, scorching my mouth all the way down to my groin. My hands find the back of her neck, fingers twisting the length of her glossy hair. She murmurs something indistinguishable into my mouth, and I gather she likes it.

Reluctantly, I pull back and break our kiss. 'We're in Dubrovnik, not Amsterdam.' I'm reminding myself more than her. She laughs and falls into line beside me, taking my hand. We stroll in comfortable silence, absorbing the scenery until we reach a beachfront hotel. Queen-sized sunbeds, enormous hammocks hanging from palm trees and makeshift private circular booths. Waiters in crisp white shirts and black shorts carry trays of multi-coloured cocktails. I might have the hangover from hell by six o'clock, but it's the perfect spot for date number three.

CHAPTER TWENTY-TWO

EMMA

Eddie whispers something into the waiter's ear and slips him some cash. He guides us to the far side of the beach, to a private alcove. It's sheltered from sight by a large semi-circle of closely planted swaying palm trees, though not shaded by them. A firepit sits in front of an L-shaped wooden couch covered with plump honey-coloured cushions. The turquoise sea laps against the shore fifteen feet in front of us. The gentle waves are the only soundtrack to our third date. Eddie nods his approval and takes the menu that's handed to him.

'More champagne? Or shall we stick with cocktails?' He really is pulling out all the stops. He doesn't have to. I like it, don't get me wrong, but I don't want him to feel like he still has to make it up to me because of what happened. If I can't understand why he did what he did, then I don't deserve to be dating him. And apparently, I am dating him. I can barely hold back the 'holy fucking shit' that dances on the tip of my tongue as the reality of the situation sinks in.

'Maybe a cocktail...' We squash on to one cushion, despite

the size of the sofa. He puts his arm beneath my knees and swings my legs up over his thighs, resting a hand on my leg. Those light, but incessant circular strokes drive me half-demented with lust.

The waiter takes our order and swiftly returns with two glasses of fruity pink liquid and a bowl filled with juicy straw-berries and chopped mango. He hands Eddie a buzzer. 'Press this if you need anything. Otherwise, you won't be disturbed.' I watch his retreating back.

And then there were two.

Eddie raises his glass and clinks it softly against mine. 'Cheers. To second chances.'

'To The One That Got Away,' I joke.

'To date three,' he murmurs seductively.

'So are we going to talk about the girlfriend remark?'

'It was the easiest explanation.'

The reverberation of my flinch shudders through both of us in this close proximity. 'I see.'

'Oh shit, Emma, I didn't mean it like that. It was easier than the truth, and I'm hoping it will be the truth...I didn't mean to be presumptuous, to put a label on us. Although you should probably get used to being labelled if you are going out with me. The tabloids love exploiting us. The first time I bring you to a restaurant, I guarantee you it will be in the papers, everyone will want to know who you are. The media aren't always kind either. It's one of the true downsides to my job.'

'I thought you liked the papers; you were in them often enough with Maria?' I can't help but ask. For a man who claims to hate the limelight, he's certainly had his fair share of it.

'Maria thrived on being on the front page. If she had no news, she'd make some up. I honestly hate it. I despise the way the media twist everything. I tend to avoid them at all costs.'

I'm struggling to ascertain his intentions. He's been saying sorry since he sat next to me on the flight two days ago. At some point, if we are going to progress, I'm just going to have to get over my previous hurt and trust him not to take off on me again.

He swings me up onto his knee, placing my legs either side of him so I'm straddling him. Only his shorts and my bikini bottoms are between us. I've never been more aware of myself. A hardness beneath me assures me the feeling is reciprocated.

I want to trust him, to believe him, but it doesn't come easily.

He pushes my sunglasses up on top of my head, and his lust-filled eyes stare intensely into mine. 'I'm mad about you, Emma.' The sincerity of his tone rings through me, striking a home run. There's an earnestness in his eyes that leads me to succumb, to believe him. After a moment's hesitation, I realise I have no option. I have to go with this, see where it takes us. Or else I'll be left forever wondering.

'Whose idea was it to leave the privacy of our own hotel room for the day?' he murmurs, shifting me an inch higher on top of his shorts. He feels so good.

I rock subtly back and forth, so subtly that it would be unnoticeable to any passer-by, not that there are any. A low groan escapes his lips, and his head lolls back on the couch.

'Emma Harvey, I'm going to burst if you continue like that.'

'You put me here,' I remind him. 'Want me to get off?' I look down into his blackening eyes.

'Don't even think about it.' His hands grip my waist, encouraging a gentle rhythm and heat pools between my legs. He's not the only one threatening to spontaneously combust with desire. There's not a soul in sight, but we are outdoors.

Anyone could arrive at any minute. And what a headline that would make, especially for a man that claims to hate the attention.

His hand returns to my thigh, where my dress has hitched up in a very unladylike manner. He sits up straighter and pushes me back an inch, questioning eyes gaze into mine. I think I know where his fingers are heading, and despite the risk of getting caught, I don't stop him. Hungry eyes scan the area behind us, a final check we are alone, before he pushes my dress up, revealing my bikini bottoms.

'I want you.' His fingers circle my inner thigh, inching closer for where I'm silently begging him to touch. With the sun scorching my bare shoulders and the chance of getting caught only adding to the excitement, he'll barely have to touch me.

I deliberately let the straps of my dress lower again, and his eyes fall onto my half-exposed breasts.

'You know exactly what you're doing to me, don't you?' His pelvis tilts up in a demonstration.

'I do.' It comes out as a whisper. 'I'm going to make sure you are never able to leave me alone again.'

His finger slips inside my bikini and slides the length of the most intimate parts of me. A gasp falls from my lips, and a lopsided grin extends all the way to his espresso-coloured eyes. He has me exactly where he wants me, stroking, pushing, teasing. Watching on, he basks in the effect he has on me. I spread my legs further, allowing him better access, and he circles my centre. The pressure's building unbearably, I'm teetering close to the edge, but I hang on, desperate to prolong the moment. It's like he knows. 'Give it up for me,' he urges, and I do, my head rolling backwards as I explode into a delicious, earth-shattering release.

His eyes burn hungrily into mine. I've never been so turned on in my life.

'Let's go for a dip.' At least under the water, I can give him what I've been dying to give him since the last time he took it.

My legs tremble with the aftershock as he lifts me gently off his lap and removes his T-shirt, holding it casually in front of him as he walks the few metres to the sea. Only when he's scanned the area again, does he throw the shirt onto the beach, revealing the obvious bulge in his shorts that he was trying to hide. He beckons me into the glistening waves.

I pull my dress up over my head and fling it on the couch, fighting the urge to sprint to where he's already chest-deep in the Adriatic. His powerful arms extend, and I dive into them. Under the warm blanket of water, I wrap my legs around his waist.

'It looks like I owe you one.' I wink at him knowingly.

'You owe me nothing.' His hands grip my bum and pull me in closer to him, grinding against him, up and down, in line with the gentle swaying motion of the waves. I glance back at the beach in the distance. People lounge obliviously on sunbeds. I can't make out their faces, so I'm pretty sure they can't see what I'm about to do. I'm not sure I'd stop even if they could see; it's gone too far now.

Lowering my legs tightly around Eddie's thighs, I shimmy back enough so I can undo his shorts and free him. A low moan rumbles in his throat. His hands cup my breasts. I move my bikini bottoms to the side and slide onto him, giving in to what I knew, deep down, was inevitably going to happen again, once our paths crossed consequentially at the airport.

Darkening eyes burn intensely into mine, his lust matching my own. He meets each grind of my hips, with a thrust of his own, losing himself deeper inside me. His fingers dig into my backside as our rhythm quickens, the sensation building again. I arch myself against him and bury my face into his enormous chest as I come undone. He follows shortly after, gripping the cheeks of my bum and releasing a prolonged noisy exhale. I balance on him, weightless in the water as he holds me in an affectionate embrace. I almost have to pinch myself.

'Holy fuck, Emma, that was hot,' he pants.

'Best third date ever?'

'Without a doubt.'

And it's not over yet.

CHAPTER TWENTY-THREE

EDDIE

Back in our room, Emma lies peacefully beside me, her glossy hair tangled over the pillow. Her naked chest gently rises and falls as she sleeps. A stray strand of hair grazes her closed eye, and I sweep it back from her face, any excuse to touch her. If I thought the first night was memorable, today blew everything out of the water, literally.

We are meeting the others at a bar called Buza, in the old town in half an hour. After today's excitement, I'd be happier not to. Sadly, that's not an option. The boys will kill me if I don't make an appearance at some point today. We are here for Callum, after all. It's just an added bonus that I've been reunited with Emma in the process.

I scroll through forty-six emails on my phone while I wait for Emma to rouse. The auction ends tomorrow at ten a.m. That's eleven here with the time difference. Keira's quiet, so I can only assume things are under control. Somebody wants that place almost as much as I do. I'm going to make certain they don't get it.

Emma stirs, turning into me, placing an arm around my waist, burying into my chest. I glance down at her face, so serene, not a line of worry anywhere. I hate to think of the hurt I caused her last September and vow internally never to hurt her again.

After the events of the last year, I never imagined I'd ever feel true happiness again. Today, I do. With Matthew's return approaching and the prospect of having our family together again, things are looking more hopeful than I could have dreamt.

'What time is it?' Emma rubs her face sleepily against my torso.

'Almost nine.' I trace a finger the length of her spine and watch as her nipples harden in response. Her eyes gleam from beneath her eyelashes; she looks at me like a lioness might look at her prey.

'I've got a feeling we're going to be late.' She pushes me flat on my back and mounts me.

'You are insatiable, woman.' It's not a complaint.

'I'm making up for the last year.' Her hips straddle me, but I gently grip her wrists and flip her onto her back, pinning her arms above her head. Tackling Emma Harvey could be my new favourite sport. From the grin on her face, she appears to feel the same.

My mouth finds hers before working downwards, over her slender neck, inching downwards. She shivers as I run my tongue below her breasts, across her stomach and down to her most intimate parts.

'Eddie,' she murmurs, running her fingers through my hair.

I don't stop until she comes undone. The sound of my name from her lips is the most sensual thing I've ever heard. Her fingers grip my biceps and urge me upwards, on top of her. I don't hesitate, sliding into my new favourite place in the world.

'You are so beautiful.' I mean it. Here like this, naked underneath me, I've never seen her look so appealing.

Her hips rock against mine, the pressure building, tight-ening. I try to hang on, but the sensation's overwhelming every inch of me. Her fingers dig tightly into my shoulders, and she moans, arching her back, and I drive into her, giving everything I've got.

My head falls on to her chest. I'm careful not to put my fifteen stone weight on her as our ragged breathing attempts to regulate again.

'You are something else, you know that?' I'm never letting this woman out of my life. It's early days, I know, but this is better than anything I've known before. It's not just the sex. There's an inexplicable comfort from her company. I hurt her more than I knew and yet she's still here, giving herself to me, openly.

'You're not bad yourself, Eddie Harrington. But if we don't get a move on soon, it won't just be your teammates you'll have to answer to. It will be mine as well.'

'I didn't know you played sport.'

'If you count drinking cocktails, I do.'

———

Buza Bar is not somewhere I would have imagined Callum picking. It's on the street parallel to Stradun, where Emma and I came the first day sightseeing. It's far from fancy, but apparently, it's the place to be in Dubrovnik on a Monday night. Locals make up the vast majority of drinkers. The paved flooring and sandy brick decor inside mirrors the image of the city walls outside. A sign on the wall reads, '*Alcohol won't fix your problems, but neither will milk.*'

I drop an arm protectively around Emma as we push

through a loud crowd of Croatian men to reach Marcus, Nathan, Ollie, Alicia, Kerry, Karen and her girlfriend. There's no sign of Callum and Abby. Our friends stare openly at us, but not one of them look particularly surprised. Wolf whistling ensues from Marcus; Nathan slaps me hard on the back. Karen yanks Emma away to undoubtedly interrogate her, as I am about to be interrogated myself.

'Well, well, well. You look like a man that's got a story to tell us,' Marcus bellows.

Subtlety never was his strong point.

'No stories here.'

There have been plenty shared between all of us over the years. Women are one of the hottest topics of conversation in the locker room, second only to the game we'd just played. Emma's too precious to discuss. The unwritten rule is, if we don't talk about our women, it's potentially serious.

'Fucking hell, he means business,' Nathan says.

'You're no joke, Eddie. You arrive in this country barely split from one girl, and you're taking another one home.' Marcus winks at the lads, stirring the pot as usual.

'Don't fucking remind me. What's the drink like?' I notice the boys are clutching pints of locally brewed lager.

'It's okay,' Ollie lies, his crinkling face gives him away.

I order a pint of it anyway and a cocktail for Emma. We exchange an intimate glance as her fingers brush over mine when she takes the glass, but it's clear that we won't be getting to spend too much time together for the next couple of hours at least.

Callum and Abby enter the bar, with James and Nadine following closely behind them. I'm so grateful they made it. Otherwise, I'd have had no other reason to stay in Emma's room.

'Sorry we're late.' Callum rolls his eyes to the ceiling and fist pumps each of us in turn. 'My mother-in-law wanted us to sit drinking brandy with Barry, Abby's third cousin twice removed. And they say weddings bring out the best in people…' Callum shakes his head and imparts a parting slap on his fiancée's bum as she heads over to where the girls congregate five feet away from us.

'Families hey. Your own is bad enough, then you get married and inherit another fucking crazy bunch.' Marcus shakes his head in apparent wonder. For a split second, I wonder if he and Shelly have had a disagreement; if that's why she isn't here. He said she couldn't make it, but he never offered a reason, and until now, it didn't occur to me to ask.

I've never had a problem with my family. I'm lucky, I suppose. Mam had four of us in six years, Matthew first, then Keira, then me, then Amy. As kids, we fought like hell, but as adults, we've always got each other's backs. We grew up with nothing, in a rough area of Dublin, but my parents worked hard, both of them, and eventually, Dad got a permanent job with the railway company and things improved hugely before I got to secondary school.

Amy is a physiotherapist, Keira is a partner in her own law firm, and until last year Matthew had a high flying marketing job with an American beverage company.

Mam and Dad live in the house we grew up in. Dad has never missed one of my matches, but things have been tense since last year. I know he blames me for what happened with Matthew, and he's right. I was driving; it was my fault. I'm hoping when Matthew comes home, and the kids are all around us, things will get back to some kind of normal, albeit a new normal.

I wonder briefly what Emma's family are like. She already mentioned her mother is cold. She'll certainly get a warm welcome from my mad lot. They'd love nothing more than to see me settle down. My sisters will appreciate Emma's direct, sharp sense of humour, not entirely a million miles from their own.

'Hey, are you even listening, lover-boy?' James gives me a swift dig in the ribs, and I realise I haven't heard a word they'd been saying.

'Sorry, what?' I zone back in as they stare at me intently.

'Is Emma coming to the game on Sunday?' The question is about so much more than the game. Bringing a girl to the game means that she's a keeper. It's more significant than bringing a girl to meet your parents for the first time, because once she gets into the player's lounge, she's actually meeting all of our parents.

I am definitely bringing her, but do they need to know that right now? I prefer to keep my cards close to my chest with this information. It's too new, too precious. The last thing I need is our relationship to become public knowledge. Not that I don't trust them, because I do. But if Maria gets wind of it, it'll look terrible. My family have always been super supportive of any negative press concerning me, but I still haven't even told them that Maria and I broke up, let alone that I'm seeing someone else. The one thing Dad raised us to believe in, is that we don't mess women around.

'We'll see.' I take a mouth of the Croatian lager. It's rotten, but not nearly as rotten as the look that Abby is throwing me from four feet away, clearly having heard the entire conversation. She understands the significance of the game as much as the lads.

'A word, please, Eddie.' She pulls me to the side, on the pretence of getting some fresh air.

We head out into the starry night. Locals call back and forth to each other, smoking cigarettes under the moonlight.

'Walk with me for a minute.' It's not a question.

'I don't know what happened with you and Emma today,' she begins, thoughtfully. 'She looks happier than I've ever seen her. In five years, I've never known her to leave the house without a full face of make-up on. Yet tonight, she's here, smiling from ear to ear without so much as a bit of lip gloss. You might not see the significance of that, but I do. It's woven into my inescapable shrink abilities. The girls tease her relentlessly for being vain. She's not vain. She's vulnerable underneath that confident exterior. Yet she arrived here with you, displaying a newfound confidence.

'You might not realise it, but you nearly broke her the last time. She's ruthless in business, but for some reason, when it comes to you, she's like putty. Don't hurt her, Eddie.'

I find myself standing at the Onofrio fountain once again, staring at those dribbling faces. The night is warm, but a shudder runs through me. I didn't realise that not wearing any make-up was the way a girl shows they are relaxed with a guy. I thought we were just rushing out the door because we'd got delayed having another bout of mind-blowing sex. But it makes perfect sense. She's relaxed around me. We've both seen each other's truths. Hers physically, mine mentally, well almost. I flinch as the demon reminds me Emma hasn't properly seen my truths, not all of them anyway.

The last few days have been the best of my life, today especially. But even with the best intentions, how the fuck can I keep my promise not to hurt her when I unintentionally tarnish everything I touch?

CHAPTER TWENTY-FOUR

EMMA

A live band begin playing deafeningly from the corner of the bar. I glance around to check on Eddie, but he's nowhere to be seen. The humidity is unreal. Bodies press and jostle hotly against one another. Karen catches me by the hand.

'Are you okay?' she shouts over an acoustic version of 'You've Got the Love'.

'Never better.' The glow on my face is an advertisement for today's activities. If only I could bottle that and sell it, I'd never need make-up again, and my new business would be worth a fortune.

'I haven't seen you looking so fresh-faced since you were fifteen. You are glowing with the look of love. Just be careful,' Karen urges, pursing her lips together in a fine line.

'I'm a big girl. Don't worry about me.' The hint of a frown forms under Karen's fringe; she's not entirely satisfied with my answer.

Kerry leans in. 'Did you get any pictures?'

Of the Elafiti Islands? Was I supposed to have?

'What pictures?'

'For *the* collage?' Kerry squeals and throws back her head with girlish laughter.

Realisation dawns on me. Even if I had taken a picture of Eddie Harrington's dick, there is no way it's going on any collage. I'm really hoping it's going to be for my eyes only from now on.

'Such a shame! Holly will be so disappointed you didn't return the favour.'

'Ha. I don't think Holly's the only one. I hope your boyfriend is due leave soon, because you are like a bitch in heat at the minute, my friend.' I take a sip of my drink and scan the bar again. Eddie is nowhere to be seen. A niggle of panic sets into my gut. Where could he have gone?

I glance around at our group to see if anyone else is missing, grateful to see that Alicia is still with us. I know she had her sights set on him yesterday, and even after today's events, I'm not entirely secure in our new relationship yet, if that's what it even is. Callum glances over at us and mouths 'Where's Abby?' and I know then I have nothing to fear.

Abby arrives back at the bar two minutes later, kisses Callum on the cheek and returns to us. Eddie follows in shortly after.

'Are you okay?' I mouth. His outstretched fingers brush over my waist as he passes by, offering the slightest nod and a smile that doesn't quite reach his eyes. Abby must have given him a rollicking, the poor fella.

I turn my attention to Abby, who looks stunning in a baby pink shirt dress. I can't forget why we are all here. It's her big day. It should be all about her, not me and Eddie.

The band belt out some classic tunes from the nineties. Abby has an ear for music, being a DJ. 'Great spot. How did you find this place?' I ask.

'The waiter, Jacov, recommended it. Said they have live

music seven nights a week. I won't be going too far tomorrow night. I'll need my beauty sleep.'

'You will be absolutely stunning. You always are.' I squeeze her hand. 'I cannot wait to see you get your happy ever after.'

James buys shots for everyone and passes them around. I notice Eddie doesn't drink his. He probably has one eye on the game on Sunday. Marcus shouts over the music, telling everyone how it's thanks to him and the bet he instigated with Callum that we are all here tonight. I am grateful for him, so unbelievably grateful, but I would be more so if he'd stop talking and let us head back to The Oceania.

Eventually, a minibus from the hotel arrives to pick us up. It's almost two o'clock in the morning and I'm ready to pass out with exhaustion that has more to do with the physical activities of the day than a need for sleep.

Abby sits in the seat in front of us, resting her head on Callum's shoulder. Karen and Fran sit to the left of us, and the rest of the gang take over the back two rows.

Eddie leans down and kisses my forehead. He's quiet tonight, all his usual humour absent.

'Are you ready for bed?' I whisper.

'You're not going to make me sleep on the couch tonight,' his hand traces up my thigh suggestively, 'are you?'

'No chance.'

The minibus parks outside reception, and we bid our friends goodnight.

'See ye for breakfast,' Eddie says.

'Yeah, if you resurface by then, Romeo.' Marcus sniggers.

The sound of my flip flops thwack against the marble floor, echoing around the otherwise quiet reception area.

'Eddie Harrington?' The receptionist calls from behind the counter. Both of us stop in our tracks; surprise and a hint of alarm creep into Eddie's cautious eyes.

'You received a fax.' She stands up and reaches for the paperwork behind her, and passes an envelope to him.

He rips it open in front of both of us, scattering minute scraps of paper in his wake. A smile extends from the corners of his mouth, all the way to the creases at the side of his eyes.

'It's from my sister. It's the paperwork for Matthew's house. It's just a matter of hours now.' He glances at a chunky silver watch on his left wrist, and I get a glimpse of the writing on the page. One word jumps out at me. Balbriggan.

A thrilling surge of excitement passes through me. It looks like Eddie and I are going to be neighbours. For some reason, I was under the impression he lived near Phoenix Park. Maybe he moved. I've been so wrapped up in our whirl-wind rekindled romance, it didn't occur to me to ask. When the holiday is over, there will be plenty of time to see his place. Even more so, now we are going to be neighbours. I can't hide the smile from my face. He thinks I'm happy for him. I am, but more so because I know we are going to be closer than I'd dared to hope.

It reminds me to pull out my phone and text Sarah. Despite the late hour, I know she'll be up early and waiting.

Hope you have the alarm set. Put the offer in at 9.50 a.m. I'll be beside the phone.

CHAPTER TWENTY-FIVE

EDDIE

Even with the comfortable bed that I'm now allowed to sleep in, I wake again at six a.m. After tossing and turning for an hour, I throw on my gym gear and creep quietly out of the room.

After an intense session sweating sheer alcohol from yesterday indulgences, I make my way to the reception area and ask them to arrange room service; breakfast in bed for two. We need to make the most of the little luxuries right now, because in a few short days, we'll be back in Dublin, both tied to strict work and training schedules, and all of this will be a distant dream.

When I return to the room, Emma is star-fished across the bed, face down, the lightest sheet covering only her bottom half. Her hair is tousled over her shoulders, and her face rests on the back of her hand like she's posed for a modelling shoot. A smile inches into the corners of my mouth as I recall why she needs the rest. Perching on the edge of the bed, I watch as her eyes begin to flutter open.

'That's kind of creepy, you know.' She stretches, stifling a yawn with the back of her hand.

'You should have seen what I was doing to you before you woke up.'

'If it was anything like last night, why didn't you wake me?'

I lean over and kiss her mouth.

'Seriously, I was in the gym. Breakfast is on the way up. Do you want to eat outside, on the balcony?'

'That sounds lovely. What time is it?' She sits upright and scrambles around for her phone.

'It's ten forty-five. I'm going for a shower.'

'Don't take too long.' She shoots me a seductive smile and flops back onto the bed.

The heat of the shower scalds my skin, but I feel great, newly optimistic. I'll be happier again when I sign this contract and send it back, knowing that Matthew's house is secured and I can begin the process of making it wheelchair friendly.

The sound of voices trickles through the running water, and I switch off the shower to listen. Emma's on the phone.

'Is it done?' Her voice is low and urgent. A sliver of alarm runs the length of my spine at her hushed demand.

There's a pause while she lets whoever she's talking to answer her question.

'I need that property. The entire new business depends on that location. Let me know if anything changes. Do not take your eye off your phone a second.'

Silence again. I don't mean to be eavesdropping, but there are no doors. If it was that private, she could have gone outside

'Only a few more minutes to go. Keep the focus, and we'll soon be celebrating. Talk soon.' In the mirror, I watch her throw the phone down onto the bedside cabinet, grin and throw back the sheet.

An uneasiness sweeps in over my stomach. I can't quite put my finger on it. Emma said there are only a few more minutes to go until she secures her new business location. It seems like an awful coincidence that the auction of Matthew's house also closes momentarily. Or do all auctions close on a Tuesday morning, at ten a.m. in Dublin?

Before I can contemplate it properly, there's a knock on the door. Emma pulls on my shirt and opens the door to a waiter wheeling a trolley full of food. As they exchange pleasantries, she points him over to the sliding doors, where he sets the small outside table with cutlery and condiments while discussing the trivialities of the weather.

I dry myself, throw on a pair of shorts and join them. The view from the balcony almost winds me. For a second, I forgot where I was, how stunning it actually is. The sun warms my face, seeping into my pores therapeutically. I'm unable to shift the chill that has inched into my bones.

It's a coincidence. It has to be.

After what seems like an eternity, the waiter leaves. Emma sits, cross-legged in the sunshine, wearing only her sunglasses and my rugby shirt, picking at fresh fruit from an exotic platter in front of her.

'Sit. Eat,' she urges. 'All that sexercise would give a person an appetite.'

I perch on the chair next to her, in mental no man's land, uncertainty drilling away at me. She lifts the crisp white linen from above the trolley and hands out a plate of sausages, eggs, hash browns and black pudding.

'What are we doing today?' She tilts her head to the side and takes a large chunk of mango.

I can't even answer her, not trusting myself to blurt out what I heard.

'Eddie? Are you okay?' She leans forward, pushes her sunglasses up on top of her unruly chestnut locks, and squints at me. 'You kind of look like you've seen a ghost.'

I'm saved from answering by the loud ringing of my mobile from inside the room. I dart inside to see Keira's number on the screen.

'Hello?' Even I recognise the urgency in my tone.

'Someone put a sneaky last-minute bid in. I just wanted to keep you in the loop, seeing as it's your money. I've placed a counter bid, but this could get very expensive, very quickly.'

I bring the phone back out onto the balcony with me, where Emma swallows a mouthful of chopped mango, oblivious to the situation that I'm ninety-five per cent sure we are entangled in. Her parting words fly through my mind. *I need this property.*

The trouble is, so do I.

I hesitate, deliberating for a few seconds.

'Eddie, are you still there?' Keira says down the phone. 'I can help you, you know, if money is a problem. I want Matthew to have that house as much as you do. I have money tied up in a few assets. I could probably work something, free up a few hundred grand, if it helps.'

'No.' That's the last thing I want. Money isn't the problem.

The problem is the woman sitting across from me, and the fact that I'm halfway to falling in love with her. If this is what I think it is, we are about to be spectacularly ripped apart.

'Do what you have to do. Whatever it takes. The money isn't a problem. Matthew needs that house.'

Emma's head whips up as I hang up the phone.

'Is everything okay?' she asks.

I wonder whether to voice my concerns. Hell, maybe she knows? Could this be her way of getting back at me for last year? It was only last night that Abby warned me that Emma was ruthless. Could she be deliberately fucking with me? To get me back for the way I treated her?

Her hand reaches out to my arm, concern in her enormous eyes. No, this has to be a massive coincidence. We must be bidding on two separate properties that just both happen to be near the beach. I take a deep breath and exhale slowly, but before I can open my mouth to say a word, her phone rings from its position on the table between us. A ridiculous rendition of Beyonce's 'Single Ladies' fills the air. The irony isn't lost on me.

'Sorry,' she says before putting one finger over her mouth to silence me while she takes the call, leaping three feet in the air in her urgency to answer it. I haven't been silenced since I was about twelve years old. It stings. I'm in two minds to get up and leave her to it, but the niggling curiosity implores I sit this out, see if it's what I think it is.

I don't have to wait long.

'Tell me,' she demands from whoever she's talking to.

I can hear a woman's voice echoing down the phone, but I can only get the odd words: *offer, outbid. Balbriggan. How far can we go?*

My guts twist in agony. My worst fears are confirmed. She eyes me from across the table. My pain must be etched obviously into my facial expression because in that split second, realisation hits her. I see it in her narrowing, darkening glare. She knows.

Her words hurt me as much as her icy penetrating stare, which sends tiny hairs electrically jolting upwards on the back of my neck.

'Do it. Whatever it takes,' she orders into the phone and hangs up.

CHAPTER TWENTY-SIX

EMMA

His nostrils flare, and black pupils burn through to my core. Emotions flit over his face like a PowerPoint slideshow; hurt, disgust, anger, determination, despair.

Adrenaline courses through my veins, igniting every fight or flight reaction I possess. I'm grateful for it. Because without my anger, I've an awful feeling I'd be enveloped by a soul-shattering sadness.

Was this entire relationship a game to him? Has he been messing with me the whole time? Using me for sex while plotting to sabotage my business behind my back? Not enough that he nearly broke me last year. He has to do it properly this time around. The fruit I've barely swallowed churns in my stomach, swirling and bubbling, threatening to make an embarrassing reappearance.

'Did you know?' His voice is choked with distrust.

'Don't you dare turn this around on me. How could you do this to me? You know that property means everything to me. I've got so much riding on this, months of product trials, testing, legislation, planning, everything.' My voice cracks, and I swallow down the emotion. The last thing I want is him to see me bawling like a baby.

The spa represents something emotionally significant to me, as well as projecting a very rewarding financial turnover. It's also my quiet demonstration that having a loving husband, the perfect 2.4 children, and a house with the white picket fence, is not the only means of achieving success.

Though, am I trying to prove it to the world? To my mother? Or to myself? With Paul's cutting remarks still occasionally echoing through my ear, I can't help but wonder.

'How could *I* do this to *you*? You have got to be kidding me! I tell you about a house five doors down from me that I'm going to buy for my disabled brother, and then all of a sudden, some mysterious buyer starts bidding against me. Are you trying to fucking hurt me, Emma? Is this because of what I did to you? I heard you were ruthless, but fucking hell, I didn't expect this.' He runs a hand through his hair and exhales a long, low sigh.

Ruthless, from anyone else's mouth, might be considered a compliment. From Eddie, it stabs through my shattering heart, more excruciatingly than a blunt rusty screwdriver.

'Eddie, I have had my sights set on that specific property since I heard it was coming to auction six weeks ago. I've been scouring the county for something beachfront, with enough space and capacity. I didn't realise you lived five doors down. Because funnily enough, I've never been to your house, probably because after you slept with me, you ghosted me.' My cheeks are ablaze with frustration and despair. My mouth is running away with itself. I should stop before I say something I regret, but I can't fight the scarlet haze coursing through me like a derailing freight train.

'Believe me, if I knew you lived there, it might have even put me off. You know my entire business is riding on this. I have ten thousand units of new products made up. I've issued employment contracts to fifteen new members of staff, in addition to the forty-three girls I already have on my payroll. I have the outdoor hot tubs ordered and the internet plagued with teaser trailers about this brand-new seaside spa that I am opening in three months, and right now, because of you, I have *no* fucking seaside spa.'

'Business, that's all it comes down to with you, isn't it, Emma?' His accusatory tone rips through me.

'In case you haven't noticed, Eddie, my businesses are all that I have.' The legs of the chair screech against the balcony floor as I push fiercely back from the table and rise, never more conscious of the fact that I'm wearing nothing bar Eddie's shirt.

'By all means, it's yours. I can't compete with your brother's needs. He deserves it way more than I ever could. It's not him I begrudge. I'm only sorry *you* didn't have the balls to tell me that you were bidding against me.'

I can't go up against him, not now I know who he's buying it for. And financially, I can't stretch any further, even with a new business loan. He could bid me under the table with his salary.

I flee the balcony, seeking solace in the shower because it's the only space in the suite that has a door that I can close, and even at that, it's see-through. The water runs over my hair and into my eyes, mingling with the fat tears rolling down my face.

For a split second, I'd dared to believe I might just be able to have it all. With the business expanding, and the way things were going with Eddie, I really thought maybe this time, just maybe, it was my time to shine. Now it looks like I have neither.

My trembling hands lather shampoo through my hair, mechanically going through the motions, my brain re-running every conversation we'd had over the last three days. Could it really be a coincidence? Either way, one of us will lose in this little game we have knowingly or unknowingly been playing. The stakes are more than just our hearts.

The worst thing about the entire ugly episode is that as bad as I feel about losing the property, the thought of losing Eddie Harrington for the second time is the one that genuinely devastates me.

I step out of the shower, wrapping the towel tightly around my body, tucking it securely under each arm, not wanting to give Eddie any more of me than he's already taken. The swirling steam leaves me momentarily blinded; I'm unable to even make out his outline. The silence is deafening. I take a deep breath and prepare myself to face another onslaught of abuse, disappointment or disgust. I'm not used to shouting. Where I grew up, voices were never raised. No, you'd have to feel passionate about something to raise your voice. Low, snide slithering remarks were far more effective in our house.

The steam eventually evaporates, waning out of the bathroom archway, disappearing up into the double-height ceiling. I needn't have worried what Eddie might say to me. Because he is gone. And so are all of his things.

CHAPTER TWENTY-SEVEN

EDDIE

My temper was quick to flare, but by the time I've unpacked my few measly belongings in my new single bedroom, I've calmed down again. The room feels huge even though it's miles smaller than the honeymoon suite. It's desolate without Emma. I even miss tripping over her mismatched shoes strewn haphazardly across the floor.

Keira's email pings through, confirming what I already know – the property is mine. Well, it's Matthew's. The joy that I hoped to feel signing that paperwork is replaced with misery. We could have a hundred happy family gatherings there, and all I will feel is Emma's absence.

While the rest of the gang congregate around the pool, I hit the beach, running eighteen kilometres in the sweltering sun, anything to take my mind off this awful gut-wrenching situation. I spend the day avoiding Emma, avoiding everyone in fact, though I can't avoid them tonight. It's the wedding rehearsal dinner, and I have to be there.

Glancing at my sorry-looking reflection in the bathroom mirror, I shave the stubble which dots my haggard face.

She may never forgive me for taking that property from under her nose, though I hope in time, she begins to understand some of my reasoning, if not the full truth of it. It wasn't out of malice, quite the opposite, in fact. I will never be able to erase the image of the hurt on her face when she realised what I'd done, made immeasurably worse by my foolish accusations that she'd done it on purpose to get back at me for ghosting her. I wince as I recall the awful truth of what I said to her, how ridiculous I must have sounded, how self-absorbed, self-centred.

She was ruthless.

She put business before everything.

But the worst thing was her response; her businesses are all she has.

Emma deserves so much better than me. I've always known it. Even if she could get over my accusations, our primary and predominant problem remains. I can't give her Matthew's house. He needs it, and I still can't even disclose the full truth about *why*.

It boiled down to a choice between my brother and her business. I chose my brother, determined to pay for my mistakes, to make up for what I've done. I'm paying the highest price I could imagine now. At least maybe that makes it even, some might call it karma.

I throw on a crisp, cream open-neck shirt and a pair of khaki slacks. The last thing I feel like doing is sitting through a formal dinner with forty other people, but I can't not be there. I just pray I'm not sitting anywhere near Emma. She's likely to stab me in the eye with her fork.

A soft knocking on my bedroom door sends a current of surprise swelling through me. One peep through the keyhole offers a soothing sight to my bleary eyes.

'Emma?'

She looks stunning in a gold dress highlighting her tanned shoulders, but I can't help but notice she's gone back to wearing the full face of make-up, the armour for the world. She means business.

'Eddie.' She bites her lower lip as her eyes struggle to meet mine.

'I'm sorry.' We both say awkwardly at the same time.

'I had no idea.' We both say in unison, with an identical apologetic tone.

'Can we get past this?' I ask.

'I don't know. I need time, a bit of space to get my head around this. It was such shock to find out that the person I was celebrating with was actually the one bidding against me.'

'Emma, I'm so sorry. It's just it's perfect for Matthew. I owe it to him.'

'You don't. But I understand you want to make his transition as smooth as possible.'

'I'd never deliberately hurt you. You know that, don't you?' My voice is pleading, borderline desperate.

She swallows hard. It must have taken a lot for her to come here.

'There must be something else suitable?' I scratch my chin, racking my brains.

'I've tried everywhere in Dublin. I need beachfront. It ties in with the main ingredient of my products: seaweed. I also need a view that's breathtaking enough to justify the prices I have to charge to cover my initial outlay costs.'

'Leave it with me, Emma. I promise I will find you something. Jesus, what are the chances?'

'It had to be you...'

Is she still talking about the property? I still harbour the distinct impression that I have unintentionally broken her trust. It's an impression that I loathe and am determined to fix immediately.

We head to the wedding rehearsal dinner together. Emma holds my hand, but it feels kind of stilted, awkward. Like we've agreed to forgive and forget, but we can't quite put it into practice. Or maybe it's just on me.

A waitress leads me straight into a private dining room overlooking the beach. One long table extends the length of the room; it's wide enough that you'd have to raise your voice to be heard across it and long enough that you can probably only converse with those either side of you. I head towards Marcus, Nathan and Ollie, who sit halfway down on the left. Emma heads towards her friends, Karen, Kerry and Fran. I assumed she'd come with me. I assumed wrongly.

For a couple that spent the first forty-eight hours almost completely entwined, we've now gone to having our own separate suites and eating dinner with our friends instead of each other.

'You managed to drag yourself out of bed,' Marcus bellows, slapping me on the back. 'Where's Emma?' His booming voice trails off as he takes in my haggard appearance.

'Over there...' I can't keep the note of bitterness out of my voice.

'Fucking hell, Harrington, you smashed it over the touchline, don't tell me you can't hammer the conversion now? What happened?' Nathan hunches forward conspicuously. For all the piss-taking and mucking around, these boys genuinely care.

'It's a long story. I need a drink.'

I pull out the chair next to Marcus and help myself to the tumbler of whisky in front of him. He signals two more to a passing waitress and sits quietly for once.

'Want to talk about it?' He rubs a hand over his shining bald head.

'Nothing to say. Apart from I'm treading deep water.'

I glance around the busy room. Callum nods at me from the top of the table, where he sits in an ivory throne-like chair. I ran into him briefly on the beach and told him about the house. I had to; he took one look at me and assumed someone had died.

Emma sits between Karen and Kerry, on the other side of the table, a little way up. Her cherry lips pinch into a tight expression. She's putting on a brave face. In her eyes, I relegated her to second place, left her high and dry, albeit unintentionally again.

A hollow sensation wrenches at my heart. These last couple of days have been the best of my life. If I can fix her business problem, would it be enough? Can we ever go back to plain sailing again, like yesterday on Bob's boat? Or is the damage already done – silent cracks perforating the foundation of our relationship before it's begun?

Efficient and discreet waiting staff serve the first course, some sort of smoked salmon salad. I push it around my plate. The only thing I'm able to swallow is forty per cent alcohol. The room is filled with a low hum of laughter and excitement. I can't bring myself to even try to make conversation with the boys, not until I fix this. I shoot her a tentative smile, she returns a pursed-lip kind of grimace.

The main course is a pink juicy looking duck dish, I stab my fork into it and twist it round in front of my face, admiring the colour and texture, yet I'm unable to put it into my mouth.

'You got to eat, man.' Marcus nudges me in the ribs, tucking heartily into his own dinner. 'If for no other reason, eat because you will need the energy on Sunday. We're already at a massive disadvantage because half the team's been here boozing all week. If we don't win, we'll never hear the end of it.'

I know he's right, but for once, I don't even care

Marcus excuses himself to phone Shelly, shaking his head at Nathan and Ollie as he gets up, as if to say I'm a hopeless cause. I don't need him to tell me. I already know.

CHAPTER TWENTY-EIGHT

EMMA

I'm a mess. My face feels tight from the sun despite my best efforts. Spraying my Ella & Jo hydrating mist, I patiently wait for it to work its magic on my tired-looking skin. It takes three types of concealer to mask the puffy bags, and no amount of glitter can put the sparkle back into my bloodshot eyes as I painstakingly apply my make-up for the wedding.

Falling asleep is a struggle at the best of times, but last night was horrific. I saw practically every hour on the clock. Once again, I dreamt I was on the beach looking for some-body, lost, terrified and alone. Even the bright light of day failed to relieve the strained tugging of my lonely heart.

Eddie didn't come to my room after dinner, and I didn't go to his. Even though we said we'd try to get past this, it's a hard one to swallow. I can't shake the feeling that losing the property was an omen, a sign that we aren't right for each other. He's what I want, but not only has he distracted me from my new business, he's actively obstructed its success. I know he didn't do it deliberately, but he put his brother before me. Totally understandable, given the circumstances, but will I always come second to everything in his life?

I've always felt so insignificant, classic middle child syndrome, constantly competing for my parents' attention. I had hoped that the person I settled down with would be someone that would put *me* first occasionally.

I didn't realise love would be such hard work.

Love? I catch myself for a second. Who am I kidding? It's no surprise, really. I was half in love with him from the first time I saw him. The last few days only confirmed what I had long suspected.

I grab my cosmetics case, throw in twelve brushes, ten shades of lipstick, four shades of foundation, and my favourite Aimee Connolly eye and cheek palettes. This morning I'm charged with doing the hair and make-up of the bridal party for the day.

Beyonce's 'Single Ladies' pierces the silence as I'm about to walk out the door to Abby's penthouse suite. I reach for it, thinking it might be Eddie or even Sarah. I've delegated her the task of scouring the county for another beachside property, even with the knowledge that finding something within budget is slim to none, but I can't just give up.

The caller display shows it's Holly.

She knows I'm abroad; she wouldn't ring for a chat unless something's happened. I can only assume it's more bad news. I seem to be having a streak of it at the moment. I drop my belongings on to the bed and pace the floor in anticipation.

'Hello?' My voice is thick with apprehension.

'Good morning to you too, sunshine.' Holly's youthful tone sings across the continent. She sounds super far away, the swishing of the windscreen wipers tells me she's driving and I'm on handsfree.

'Is everything okay?' I need the reassurance.

'Yessss.' She draws out the word painfully, which fills me

with doubt. 'Tell me, did you bump into Eddie Harrington on your travels?'

'It's a long story.'

'I'll pick you up from the airport, you can tell me all about it. It's Saturday, you land, isn't it?'

Now I know there's something wrong. Holly never surfaces before lunchtime on a Saturday, and even if she does, she hates driving around the city at weekends. She does enough driving during the week as a sales rep for the pharmaceutical company that she works for.

'What's going on?' I twist my finger around my loose hair and pull gently enough, so the focus is on that part of my scalp, rather than the uneasy feeling swelling in my stomach.

'Nothing...' From the way she draws the word out, I know that she's lying.

'Holly, you're worrying me. What's up?'

'It's Mam,' she admits with a sigh.

'What about her?'

'She's gone.'

'What do you mean gone?' A cold shiver runs the length of my spine despite the heat.

'She's run off with some fella from the golf club, Anthony Montgomery. Apparently, they're in love! He has a big fancy house on the southside of Dublin. She phoned me this morning and asked me to call over, said she wanted to talk to me. I thought I'd finally reached the age where I was due the "you better stop fooling around and find yourself a husband" monotone speech. Instead, I got the "I'm leaving your father speech".'

Shock paralyses my pacing. My mother? Left? That can't be right. I can't even begin to imagine it. She must have actually felt something like love, or lust at the very least in order to leave Dad for another man. Impossible to imagine when she's barely shown us any emotion throughout our entire lives.

'You can't be serious. Has our cold-hearted mother actually found someone that stirs some sort of emotion in her? He must do if she's upped and left.'

'Have you heard from Dad?' Holly asks.

'Not a thing. He's in Portugal until the end of the month. They've just started a big new construction contract. Does he know?'

'No idea. But unless he calls me, I'm waiting until you get home on Saturday to investigate.' My sisters always claim that I am my father's favourite. For a long time, I seriously doubted it because if I was, he wouldn't have left us with *her,* while he worked fifty-one weeks of the year in every country except the one in which his family lives. Mind you, as I got older and had to endure Mam's moods, it became clearer why he did what he did. Whatever she's like as a mother, I can't imagine she was ever any more loving as a wife.

I hated that he wasn't around for the day-to-day stuff growing up. I missed him, his easy laughter and his awkward dad hugs. But I never blamed him for it.

'What about Grace?' Neither of us are particularly close to our older sister.

'She's devastated. The pregnancy hormones aren't helping.'

'I can't actually believe it.' My fingers drag through my hair.

'If it weren't so freaking worrying, it might actually be funny.' A nervous laugh travels across the miles. 'Imagine her, on her high horse telling us what we should be doing, and then carrying on like a love-struck teenager behind everyone's backs.'

'Holy fuck.' A heavy breath burst from my mouth. 'So, what now?'

'Your guess is as good as mine.'

'Fucking hell, Holly. This is like a bad episode of *Fair City*.'

'Poor Dad.'

'What do you mean, poor Dad? He's finally free of the snide remarks. It might be the best thing that ever happened to him.'

'Maybe...' She's not as sure as me, but our mam treated him with the same coldness as she did me. He'd have to be a saint to put up with that.

'I'm sorry if I'm ruining your holiday, but I wanted to give you the heads up.'

'I'm glad you did. Where's Frankie?' My concern turns to my fur baby.

'I brought him with me earlier. Apparently, Anthony won't tolerate dogs at his southside palace.'

He sounds like a douche already. What kind of person doesn't like dogs?

A car horn beeps deafeningly in the background.

'Emma, I gotta go. Text me your flight details, and I'll see you Saturday. Take no crap from Harrington. Tell the girls I say hi.'

'Kerry loved your collage.' I remember wryly. 'Next time, perhaps you could just send them directly to her phone?'

She squeals with girlish laughter. 'Plenty more where those came from. Jesus, maybe even Mam will add to the collection. Yuck! Love you, byeee.'

I'm left staring down at my handset, bewildered.

I brush my hair absentmindedly, stalling for time to gather my thoughts. How could she do that to Dad? To us? Why would she put such an emphasis on her daughters getting married when clearly it made her so unhappy?

Swallowing hard, I recall how much pressure I felt to impress her with the spa and all the work that had gone into the new range. All to prove that I was worthy – because I hadn't yet made it in life as someone's wife – a title she has apparently abandoned. One rule for her, one for us. She has cut the final cord for me in some ways, yet my relief is tinged with sorrow. I might have ended up wasting a lot of money, but I no longer have to prove myself to the self-declared matriarch of our family. I gather my belongings and swallow the last mouthful of a cold cup of coffee before banging the door behind me and heading to Abby and Callum's room.

Even from behind thick solid doors, I can tell the party is in full swing already by the shrieking laughter and the distinctive pop of a bottle of something fizzy.

Mrs Queenan opens the door, with the same rollers in her hair that she'd worn for the hen night. She clutches baby Casey in one arm and a glass of champagne in the other. It's barely nine o'clock in the morning, but the suite is overflowing with our friends, merry on bubbles and excitement shining in their eyes. I plaster on the biggest smile I can muster. Noel strolls the length of the room, topping up glasses and rolling his eyes.

It's an odd moment to realise there is no such a thing as a normal family, anywhere.

CHAPTER TWENTY-NINE

EDDIE

On the white sandy beach, seventy-eight white wicker chairs with duck egg bows form symmetrical rows on either side of a white sand aisle. Callum stands tall at the front, his shoulders held back in proud anticipation. He looks smart but relaxed; barefoot, wearing navy linen shorts, a crisp white short-sleeved shirt and a duck egg corsage. The registrar stands under a large wicker archway, intricately entwined with long-stemmed white roses waiting for the bride's arrival.

As the harpist begins playing, Abby approaches the aisle, supported by her father's strong arm. She is the perfect blushing bride in a light chiffon dress. Delicate spaghetti straps grace her shoulders. The dress emphasises her slim waist before kicking out in a long skirt that trails behind her as she walks barefoot to the front.

I steal a look across the aisle, to where Emma sits, two rows back with Karen, Fran and Kerry. Bar a curt smile and a strained nod, she's barely glanced in my direction. Wearing a backless baby pink dress, she looks stunning. Her loose hair is gathered at one side, exposing a taught, tanned back. How is it even possible for a person's back to look so appealing? Emma's does. It begs to be held tightly in an embrace that I'm uncertain she'll let me give her. Not now, after everything.

Last night I rang Callum's fixer Declan and asked him to look into potential properties for me. He tried every estate agent in Dublin this morning. There is nothing in the way of beachfront properties available at the moment. One guy said he might have something next month, but what good is that? I need something now. I can't escape that sinking desolation weighing on my soul. As the distance increases between Emma and me, the pressure to fix it increases tenfold.

But I can't let Matthew down, so there's no other way.

Ollie gives me a swift dig in the ribs, as if to remind me to face forward. I focus back on the bride and groom, who gaze at each other in total adoration; their baby girl sits between them in a white pram. As they exchange the vows we are all so familiar with, a hard lump wedges in my throat, practically choking me.

There is barely a dry eye in the place. Even Marcus watches on intently, pride etched into his overbearing stance. As the couple are pronounced man and wife, their guests applaud wildly. Marcus wolf whistles next to me, the noise testing the delicate tissue of my eardrums. Smiling is infectious. Every single person here is grinning like an idiot. Some dab at stray tears, others pound their palms together in a deafening clap.

Callum closes the distance between him and Abby and kisses her like no one is watching, like they are the only two people in the entire universe. A sliver of envy eats at me, snaking its way into my stomach, travelling through my thorax and coiling around my heart. I want what he has, and I don't mean Abby. I mean the wife, the family, someone of my own; someone who knows my deepest darkest secrets and accepts me anyway.

An idea strikes like lightning from above. Emma needs a beachfront property – she can have mine! I'll happily give her my house as a gift if she'll accept it. Maybe then she will see I'm willing to put her needs before my own, elevate her onto the pedestal that she deserves to sit on. It's the ultimate gesture. And it's the best chance I've got. A tiny flicker of hope surges through me. Maybe, just maybe, I can fix this. She won't ever be able to doubt how I feel about her again. We train away at Carton House three nights a week, sometimes more, and I'm fairly sure Callum will let me crash at his empty flat, as I did when my house was being renovated last year. And if things go in the direction I hope they will, I'll be staying at hers anyway.

'You okay?' Ollie asks, a quizzical look passes over his face,

'Yeah, why?'

'It's the first time I've seen you smile in about two days,' he says.

'I've thought of a plan,' I admit, scratching my scar with my fingers in a silent 'touch wood' thing that I do. As we throw confetti at the bride and groom walking united back down the aisle together, I find myself grinning, really grinning as the idea formulates in my mind.

We gather by the pool, congregating around the two bar areas that have been set up in addition to Jacov's ivory and duck egg decorated hut. The main pool has been cordoned off for the wedding, but there are two smaller pools on-site the other guests can use. Nobody seems to mind; passers-by stop to admire the beautiful bride offering their congratulations. Most of them haven't got a clue they're actually Irish celebrities, here to avoid the press.

Waiters pass around champagne flutes, but I pass up the

offer, deciding against drinking today. It doesn't help. It might provide a short-term escape, but long-term, it makes me sluggish and slow. I need my wits about me to execute my plan. Keira's going to take a lot of convincing to do the paperwork on this one. Her maternal instincts know no bounds when it comes to her little brother. Plus, the weekend is fast approaching, and despite everything else going on in my life, I have one eye on the Munster match. The last thing I want is to compromise my position on the team. Apart from the honour it provides, if I keep giving away houses, I'm going to need the income.

After making a point of shaking Callum's hand and kissing Abby's cheek, I sneak under the shade of a parasol to type out an email to Keira. I know it's going to raise a few eyebrows. I hit send before I can overthink it. Within ten minutes, my phone is repeatedly vibrating in my pocket. I excuse myself from the conversation I'm involved in and walk towards the beach, staring at the incoming waves.

'Hello?'

'Eddie, I can't let you do this.' Keira's voice is etched with concern.

'It's not up to you. If you won't help me, I'll find a solicitor who will.' My tone is curt. I appreciate her concern, but I'm old enough to make my own decisions.

'Who is this girl?'

'It's a long story, but in short – she's The One That Got Away.' I steal the term she used to describe me because it's not only apt, it's true. A rushed explanation follows, but still, Keira's not convinced.

'Spending all your money on people you have unintentionally hurt won't change the past,' she cautions.

'I know. But it will make me feel better about it, at the very least. I need to show Emma that she means more than any other woman in the world to me.'

'Huh!' Keira huffs down the phone.

'Apart from my two darling sisters, of course,' I rectify. 'You know what I mean, though. It's okay for you, you have Dermot and the kids. I have nobody of my own. And I want her, more than ever before. The truth is she's too good for me, but I'm not prepared to lose her again. Not without a fight.'

'I hope you're right. You don't exactly have the greatest track record with women. You better hope Maria doesn't get wind of this either. She's likely to hang you for it.'

'Don't pretend you're not ecstatic to be shot of her.' Maria had only met my sister once in the player's lounge. She'd invited herself to the match, and I couldn't think of an excuse quick enough to deny her.

'She was kind of scary. Emma has to be an improvement.'

'I only hope you get to find out.' A gust of air that I hadn't realised I was holding burst out from my lungs.

'I'll have the paperwork faxed over to the hotel reception before five o'clock. I'll need Emma's full name, date of birth, PPS number and address. I hope you know what you are doing.' A gentle click signifies she's gone.

———

Emma sits at a table across the room from me. I can't catch her eye but I feel her gaze on me intermittently. I understand why she's hurting. I really do, but I'm about to fix it, win her back, and give our story an ending fit for one of those pink novels that she loves.

We gather outside again, watching the bride and groom waltz around the makeshift poolside dance floor for the first dance. Fascinators have been abandoned and ties discarded. A DJ sits in a wooden box, huge black headphones balance around his neck as he bounces to his own beat. The spectacular setting sun provides the perfect backdrop to an almost perfect day.

I stand with my teammates, watching as the women begin to congregate around Abby shrieking, arms flailing with dramatic gestures. Emma leans at the bar talking to Mrs Queenan, who seems to be nudging her in the direction of the other women, clucking and pecking in encouragement like a mother hen. I watch engrossed as Emma reluctantly hands over her drink to Abby's mother and takes her place amongst the other women.

Balancing precariously on a chair, Abby stands with her back to her squealing, jostling friends. Only when she raises a cream bouquet of a hundred roses above her head do I realise she's about to throw the bouquet. The DJ lowers the music down, and the well-oiled guests begin to clap rhythmically. Abby counts backwards, five, four, three, two, one...

Marcus stops talking and nudges me knowingly. The lads fall silent, watching the women. The bouquet glides over Abby's shoulder, cutting straight through the air. For a slim woman, she demonstrates a pretty powerful throw. The bouquet spins, and four arms jump up high to catch it. The excited squealing resumes, defying odds with an even higher pitch than before. For a second, it's impossible to distinguish who caught it. Then I see Emma, cheeks flushed, arms overflowing with roses. She looks up, glancing across the pool, and catches my eye. A bolt of lightning pierces my heart.

'Well, things are looking up for Emma, at least,' Marcus announces, rubbing his hands together with glee. 'Let's see who she gets paired off with.'

My sudden joy turns to impending doom as I see Callum picking Abby up by her waist and placing her on a chair on top of the bar, remembering that the girl who catches the bouquet will dance with the single guy that catches the garter.

He lifts up her dress enough for us to see the lace band wrapped around his wife's tanned thigh. Wolf whistles pierce the air. Noel shakes his head and takes a swig of his pint.

Before I've given it a second thought, I'm there at the front of fifteen single men. To my surprise, my teammates are with me. Are they here to help me or hinder me? Either way, when Callum throws that garter, it will be mine. I will win that dance with Emma. I'll tell her what I've done and that I'll never put her needs second again.

The DJ plays a song with a firm beat that pounds through my ears and pumps through my heart. Adrenaline spikes within. Callum's thrown me a good few passes over the years, and I've yet to miss any of them. I don't plan on starting now.

Callum licks his lips in an obvious show of appreciation for his wife, who laughs down at him. Being the showman he is, he works the crowd, dramatically taking Abby's calf in the back of his hand and planting a kiss on her silky looking skin.

'Easy lad,' Noel shouts from behind us, which provokes a ripple of laughter in the gathering crowd.

He puts his hands behind his back and runs his lips seductively up the length of her leg, grips the garter with his teeth and pulls it effortlessly down, slipping it from her ankle. The guests clap, alcohol-fuelled laughter fills the air. My eyes remain solely on the prize.

Callum is with me; he shoots me a meaningful glance, and his eyes dart very slightly to the left in an unspoken exchange that I'm exceptionally familiar with. He flings his head to the right before swinging it back again with gathering momentum and tosses the garter from his teeth into the air towards my left cheekbone. I jump into the air and grasp the flimsy material with both hands, like it's the most precious possession of my life. It was one of the quickest passes we've ever executed. My teammates applaud, jostling into me, someone ruffles my hair, another claps my back.

The sense of victory is fleeting as I see Emma staring stony-faced at me, clearly not as thrilled as I am with the turn of events. She knocks back the remaining champagne in her glass and walks reluctantly towards the makeshift dance floor to follow through on tradition and face her certain fate.

CHAPTER THIRTY

EMMA

Eddie waits in the middle of the floor. I approach, dragging my heels as the catcalls begin from the wedding crowd. I pray it's not a slow lovey-dovey song that goes on for hours. It could be anything, knowing Abby. She has an awful penchant for eighties cheese. Please don't let it be Lionel Ritchie. I can't cope. Swallowing hard, I force down the swelling apprehension bubbling in my chest. Bad enough I'm confused about Eddie, but the entire wedding watching us work it out is way too personal. At least the fading glow from the rapidly sinking sun semi-shelters my pink flushed cheeks.

The first few bars of Sam Smith's 'Stay with Me' echo through the air. Eddie stands three feet in front of me, looking almost as apprehensive as me, though I'm not sure why because he actively pursued that garter. I was simply unluckily lucky with the bouquet. Had I not raised my arms, I'd be sporting a black eye.

He closes the space between us, those huge espresso eyes burning intensely into mine in a silent apology. Sorrow, regret, maybe even a glimmer of hope flicker in the glinting of his pupils. There's little hope. I've decided to stick to my original plan, avoid men for the next three months and focus on the business. It's what I should have been doing all along, then I wouldn't have been blindsided.

Strong warm hands lightly grip my waist, and I reluctantly put my arms around his shoulders. I hate that he smashed my future, my business and our relationship to pieces in one single moment. But what I hate more is the comfort I'm getting from the pressure of his chest against mine and the security of his familiar scent – his citrus aftershave, and the smell of mint from his ragged breath. I hate the way his touch makes me tingle from my breasts to my thighs, and what I hate the most is that I can't give in to him. I can't keep being his second choice. His presence in my life is too much of a distraction. The risk is too great. The potential he possesses to hurt me is astronomical. Mimicking one of my mother's cold displays, I rearrange my features sternly to express this.

Sam Smith opens with his famous first line, something about a one night stand.

Our feet move in an automatic rhythm, right, left, right, left.

'So do it again then...' shouts Marcus from where he stands, ogling from the side-line, beer in hand, guffawing at his own joke.

Sam Smith continues crooning about needing love, regardless of the interruption.

'Make-up sex is the best sex!' Kerry shouts less than help-fully from next to Marcus. She's been on the Sea Heave again since lunchtime. Nathan stands way too close to her for comfort, he's clearly got designs on her, but he hasn't got a chance. She's been with Craig for eight years. She's not going to throw that away on a holiday fling.

Betrayingly, the tension begins to slip from my shoulders. I tell myself to enjoy this dance because it will likely be the last legitimate contact I have with Eddie Harrington. He might not have intentionally hurt me, but he's done it twice now. I need security. I need to know where I stand. I need loyalty.

Eddie tightens his grip on my waist, squeezing me further into him, before grabbing my hand and hurling me out in a giddying twirl that I can't help but smile at. He pulls me back in just as fast, staring down at me.

'I'm sorry.' It's barely more than a whisper.

'Me too.' Truly I am. It's been a crazy day but enlightening day. What with Holly's news this morning as well. I'm struggling to get my head around everything, but one thing's become crystal clear as the day has passed, the only thing I can count on right now is myself. I *have* to focus on the business. Just because the pressure is off from my mother, I plan to bull ahead with the spa, for me, for my new employees and for everyone out there that has ever doubted me.

My anger about the property has evaporated. A sinking sense of sadness settled in its place. Eddie and I are just not meant to be.

'Can we start again?' A hopeful uncertainty cracks in his low tone.

'I don't think so, Eddie. Whatever about second chances, I'm definitely not a believer in third time lucky. My heart can't take it again.'

We twirl in a silent embrace until the song finishes, all too quickly. As the final bars play out, I give him a final lingering kiss on the cheek and pull away from him. 'Goodbye, Eddie.'

He catches my hand, tugging me towards him once again. His mouth brushes my ear. 'I left a present for you behind the reception desk. When you get five minutes, go and have a look. It's the only way I can show you how much you mean to me. I can't give you Matthew's house. I promised it to him long before I knew you wanted it, but it's the next best thing... When you've had a chance to see for yourself and think things over, I'll be in the residents' bar. I hope to god we can get through this.' Expressive eyes lock into mine, ripping my heart right from my chest.

He turns away, leaving me staring at his broad, retreating back.

Loitering next to Karen and Fran, I sip on a glass of champagne, trying to hide the fact that despite my protests, yet again, Eddie Harrington just rocked my world. He's the only man I've ever encountered that is capable of creating that effect on me. Every time I think about giving up on him, he somehow draws me back in.

'Where are you going? Sneaking back to lover-boy?' Kerry grabs my arm, stopping me in my tracks. I told them about the house. I had to. It was obvious something had gone badly wrong.

'I need to make a quick trip to reception.' She doesn't need to know why. Curiosity is eating me alive.

'Yeah, yeah, that's what they all say.' Her s's are slurring, and Karen raises her eyebrows at me before holding up seven fingers behind Kerry's back. We are getting dangerously close to carnage on the Kerry-O'Metre.

Nathan arrives and asks Kerry to dance. No one could miss the way he's been looking at her the last few days, but he hasn't got a chance. I thought Ollie might have shown a bit of interest in her, seeing as he's single too, but the only thing Ollie is interested in is his phone. I slip away unnoticed.

The sharp clicking of my heels against the marble floor alerts the reception staff to my approach.

'Hi. I'm Emma, from room 425. I think you have something for me?' It sounds odd coming out of my mouth, but the receptionist is clearly used to weird requests because she simply smiles, reaches underneath the desk and presents me with a thick brown A4 envelope, which I tuck safely under my arm to open in private.

I make my way back to room 425 for a bit of privacy. Kicking off the heels, I bask in the soothing feel of the thick fluffy carpet between my squashed toes. It's eerily quiet in comparison to the raucous noise of the party.

Perching on the edge of the bed, I tear open the envelope, scanning the contents impatiently. It's a pile of formal documents relating to the Balbriggan property. I rub my temples, trying to work out what is going on. He literally just told me not fifteen minutes ago that he couldn't sell it to me. Yet it looks like a photocopy of the deeds, with my name on them, signed by a Keira Harrington, the infamous solicitor sister.

I run my finger over the lines in an attempt to locate what I'm missing here. It doesn't take long to find it. The property transferred into my name is not the original one I wanted, number two. The property, which I now apparently own, is number seven, five doors down. A gasp slips out of my mouth as clarity dawns. He couldn't give me Matthew's house, but he gave me his own.

I throw the paperwork down on the bed. I can't accept it. It's ridiculous. Eddie wanted to be close to his brother, that was the whole point. There's no way on this earth I would take that away from him. There's no way I'd even buy the original building– number two – either. Not now I know what he has planned for it.

This is utterly bonkers. I pace the floor, wondering how to transfer it back to him without looking like an ungrateful bitch. If I were to accept, I'd be forever in his debt, and that's not a great position to be in. Not with a person I'm head over heels in love with and terrified of being discarded by again. And as well-intended a gesture, as it was from Eddie, he can't buy me. I am not for sale.

I slip my swollen feet back into my stilettos, touch up my foundation and remove the mascara streaks below my eyes. I'll tell Eddie I can't accept it. I will find another beachfront property. It might delay my launch by six months, but seriously, who am I trying to impress anymore anyway?

I'm permanently striving for the next thing, the next achievement, the next string to my bow, and for what? To impress my less than loving mother? She's been lying to us all for months, if not years, and belittling Believe in Beauty at every opportunity she gets, making me feel like whatever I achieved was never good enough. It speaks volumes about her mental state. But with the news of her affair, I am free from the sense of duty to prove myself to her.

I'm only sorry it took her leaving, for me to realise that I do not need her approval, or anyone else's for that matter. Neither a husband nor a business or any property under the sun equals success. Only happiness does.

Which leads me to wonder, what *does* makes me happy? What do I want out of this life? Because there is a huge gaping void in my life that four businesses have failed to plug, so why on earth did I think the fifth would fill it? It hits me then, a flashback of the wedding, the way Callum gazed so adoringly at Abby, the way their eyes exchanged so much more than vows spoken today. That's what I want. It's what I've always wanted, and not because of some messed-up desire to please my mother.

I pace the carpet once again; it's a dreadful habit. I shouldn't have even bothered to put my shoes back on. I'm nowhere near ready to head back down yet. Something catches my eye underneath the bed as I'm midway across the room. I kneel down, stretching my arms as far as I can reach and grasping the green material in wonder. Yanking it out suspiciously, I realise it's Eddie's Ireland jersey. The one I slept in the first night. The one that he insisted I put on the night we got back from Buza Bar, so he could reenact what he claimed he should have done to me the first night.

I clutch it tightly to my face and inhale the neckline; there's still a faint trace of Eddie lingering on the collar. The scent soaks into my nostrils, weaving a sense of calm through my body and into my heart. Eddie is what makes me happy, the smell of him, the sight of him and the feel of him.

Realisation punches my gut like a sixteen stone heavy-weight boxer. I can't accept his gift, but I can accept his offer to try again. If he'll still have me. Even though he's already had more chances than any other man I've ever dated, I can't shake the feeling that he deserves one more. When I look back, none of our undoing was his doing, not intentionally anyway. Maybe there really is such a thing as third time lucky? He didn't intentionally break my trust. He helped his brother out – it wasn't like he went running back to Maria. And if this gesture is anything to go by, he *is* willing to put me first.

It suddenly dawns on me that today is the anniversary of the first time we met, the first time he kissed me, the first time we did a lot of things. Abby and Callum wanted to get married a year on from their engagement party. I can't think of a better day for the first day of our third fresh start.

CHAPTER THIRTY-ONE

EDDIE

The gentle tap on my shoulder from behind prompts a surge of hope rushing through me.

Perching on a bar stool, I swivel around with a hopeful smile. 'Shall we start over?'

I open my arms instinctively to embrace her, but the wrong woman stands before me.

My mouth drops open in unconcealable shock. Tongue-tied, I splutter and jump to my feet in an attempt to feel more in control.

'I was hoping you'd say that.' A coy smirk curls on her victorious lips.

'Maria?' I can't actually believe my eyes, but I'm definitely not hallucinating.

'*Zurprise.*' She holds her toned, tanned arms out to me and offers her brightest smile.

'But you...We...I wasn't expecting you.' My hand immediately traces the familiar line of my stubble.

'Pah! You know *vhat* I'm like, Eddie.' Her French accent

brutally accentuates each syllable. Hard to believe I'd once found it sexy. Tonight it grates my nerves like talons scraping the length of the old school blackboard.

'My temper has *zee* habit of running away *vith* itself.' She places a warm hand on my chest, yet it makes my blood run cold.

She's not supposed to be here. She finished with me, very dramatically, after I failed to remember it was the anniversary of our first tweet. Who the fuck remembers that type of shit? She's batshit fucking crazy, and when she lost it with me last weekend, all I felt was relief. Her mood swings exhaust me. I've moved so far past this, yet here she is, back for more.

The smile freezes on her face as the first hint of doubt creeps in. In her crazy mind, I should be throwing my arms around her right now and weeping with joy that she came around. Oh, I feel like fucking weeping alright, but certainly not with tears of joy. I've moved on. Realised what I actually want in life. What I need. And it's not her.

'Eddie? You are happy to *zee* me?' Cerise pink lips curl into a childlike pout, exposing razor-sharp canines that I don't wish to bear the brunt of.

I stand, mute, mouth opening and closing like a fish that's trapped in six-inch glass bowl. My usual defence of cracking a joke is certainly not appropriate in this situation. There's nothing remotely fucking funny about any of it.

'Your silence is *vorrying* me, Eddie.'

Her presence is *vorrying* me.

'Maybe you and I should find somewhere quiet to sit, Maria? So we can talk.' I point towards a dark corner with a booth before Emma sees her and get the wrong idea, and before Maria can cause one of her infamous explosive scenes. Her mood swings are almost as famous as her slice serve. I'm in no mood for them tonight, but this is not a situation I can laugh off, not if I want to maintain some level of integrity. Honesty is the only option.

Marcus enters the bar before I can hide Maria away somewhere discreet.

'Well, well, well, if isn't Hooker Harrington.' Marcus slaps me on the back, surprise alight in his eyes. Could he make it any more fucking obvious? I silently plead with him not to hang me out to dry with my recent relations with Emma.

If I can get rid of Maria swiftly, maybe I can avoid telling Emma she even arrived. It is her one wound. Whatever about the property, Maria's reappearance here is something she would never forgive.

'Marcus.' I shake hands with him and try to convey a seriousness with my stare.

'Maria, you know what the Irish say about weddings? Going to a wedding is the making of another.' Marcus winks at Maria, with his tongue protruding between his teeth. He cannot help but stir the shit. I'm going to batter him the next time we're on the pitch.

'Next thing you know, he'll be down on one knee, begging. Do yourself a favour, say no. I've seen what he looks like in the mornings. It's not pretty.' He howls with laughter as he hammers the final nail into my coffin, oblivious to the tension radiating in the air around us.

'Is Marcus right?' Maria falls into line beside me as I power walk us towards the corner of the room, where the lights are dimmest. No matter how gently I break this to her, she is going to lose her shit explosively.

'About what I look like in the morning?' Old habits die hard. I buy a few more seconds until we are far enough away not to cause a scene.

'*Vill ve* be the ones walking the aisle next?' She takes a sidewards glance at me as my heart contracts in my chest.

The thought of walking down the aisle with Maria sends tremors through my body. I'd rather walk the fucking plank.

How did I let this go on? It just demonstrates what kind of mental state I've been in since last year. Being with Emma, who is so strong, assertive and direct, has reminded me that the poor excuse of an on/off relationship with Maria severely lacked in comparison.

'Marcus is wrong.' I sigh deeply, not even bothering to sit. I clear my throat, look directly into her darting eyes, and say what needs to be said.

'We've broken up more often than we've actually seen each other. You're based in France. My home will always be Ireland. Long term, we would never have worked. I'm sorry, Maria. I thought after our split at the weekend, you'd be glad. I'm clearly not what you're looking for. If I was, there wouldn't be half as many arguments.'

'The best part of *ze* arguing is *ze* making up.' She leans in on her tiptoes towards me. I catch her loosely by the wrist, forcing her to pause.

'I can't do this anymore. I'm sorry you came all the way out here. I'll pay for any hotel in Dubrovnik for your holiday. But we can't carry on seeing each other. We are not a good fit. I'm so sorry.'

'You're *zeriously* breaking up with me?' Widening eyes fill with crocodile tears. She can turn them on instantaneously. I've seen her do it countless times over the last few months.

'Technically, you broke up with me last weekend.' I can't make it any clearer.

She places her hand over the small of her stomach and gazes up at me with a touch of defiance. 'I'm pregnant, Eddie.'

CHAPTER THIRTY-TWO

EMMA

Entering the dimly lit bar, the first person I spot is Kerry. Her left hand clings flirtatiously onto Nathan's bulging bicep, her right hand clutches what looks a tequila slammer, the lemon ready on the bar in front of them standing as proof of their drunken intentions. Nathan is probably hoping one thing will lead to another, but he's in for a shock. Craig is away a lot but Kerry has never, nor would ever, cheat on him.

I hover in the doorway, watching from afar. Kerry licks what I can only assume is salt from the back of her hand without breaking Nathan's stare. She knocks back the shot of clear liquid and expertly bites the lemon. Nathan's hands clap together before finding their way to Kerry's face. I'm certain she's about to brush him off and probably in a spectacular fashion, but it's me that's in for the shock. She submits to him, raising her hands to his neck, stretching up on to her toes to tilt her face to defiantly meet his. Nathan's lips crash down onto hers before she has the chance to change her mind. My hand clamps over my mouth, and I turn on my heels so I can deny any future knowledge of this.

Kerry's endeavours are her own business. Eddie is the sole reason I'm standing here. The thought of being back in his arms sends a dizzying wave of heat through me. Scanning the rest of the bar, I spot his broad frame right away. His muscular back is turned from me. He's talking to someone, probably another guest. Crossing the room, I'm desperate to tell him how much I care for him, how I believe not only in second chances, but third chances as well. I have every intention of throwing my arms around him and apologising, but my feet skid to an abrupt halt on the shiny tiles ten feet away from him as I notice that he's involved in an intensely animated discussion with a beautiful brunette.

Her right hand slides round his waist, pulling him towards her. My fingers clasp together until my knuckles whiten. Why isn't he pushing her away? I can't see his face, can't work out what's going on. The woman uses her left hand to grab his fingers and places them over her stomach, staking some of primal claim on him. I'm frozen to the spot, unable to watch, but unable to tear myself away as realisation strikes, cutting through me, tearing me in half.

It's Maria. She's here. Should I approach? Or slink away quietly?

So much for third time lucky. I'm frozen to the spot, unable to drag myself away from the horror show in front of me, oddly compelled to watch as the foundation of my new world cracks and crumbles around me, yet again.

I could never have competed with her. Not only does she have naturally flawless, sallow skin, but she's a fellow athlete, with a toned physique to prove it. And my Dublin twang simply can't compete with the whispering fragments of her low, sensual French accent.

At that moment, her glinting eyes flicker up to meet

mine. She flashes a victorious grin, as though she knows she is ripping my heart clean out of my chest, but how could she? I am nobody to her.

Eddie catches her stare, following her line of sight. His heavy eyebrows burrow together in what looks like dismay. He glances indecisively from her, to me and back to her again, a rabbit well and truly caught in the headlights. His mouth opens to say something but closes before the words come out. He has a decision to make. Swallowing hard, he offers one last glance at me, almost apologetically, before returning his gaze to her, his choice made, as easy as that.

She offers him a tiny affectionate nudge towards the door, gazing up at him adoringly; a woman who knows she's got her man back exactly where she wants him. A thousand daggers rupture my heart as he places a hand firmly on Maria's back and guides her out of the bar.

I run for the stairs passing by Kerry and Nathan, who are still locked in an explicit game of tonsil hockey and are thankfully oblivious to my presence, and that the world as I know has been smashed into a thousand pieces by the one man I foolishly trusted. Turns out Paul was right, life isn't like one of my crappy romance novels after all.

My heels click all the way through the marble reception. I pray I make it back to the sanctuary of my own room before the tears start. Bile presses tightly on my chest, suffocating me. I flee down the corridor, passing Abby's father in the process.

Only when I'm behind the safety of my hotel room door do I permit the tears to flood from my eyes. The sobs that escape my chest mimic that of a wild animal caught in a trap. I don't care. I don't care about anything anymore. There's no going back from this. Not ever. I've been such a fucking idiot. Sinking to the floor, I rest my back against the door for added security. Not that anyone is coming, I'm not completely delusional.

He picked her. The same three words whip around my head, piercing my heart. I can't quite believe it, yet that niggle inside warned me it would always come to this. Salty water streams from my swollen eyes until there is nothing left, apart the carcass of a woman that used to have a soul.

What a stupid fool I have been. The pain tears at my insides, but I've only got myself to blame. I knew, I always knew he would go back to her.

Hours pass motionlessly. Birds sing from the balcony reminding me I've been sat in the same position all night. Using the wall for support, I head for the shower. The fast flowing water does nothing to ease the tension in my skull and in my heart. The steam envelops me. No matter how much I scrub myself, I can't cleanse myself the way I want to, can't remove the repulsive, harrowing rejection.

Maria obviously has some sort of weird infatuating hold on him. Even with the constant fights and endless drama, he always goes back to her. I knew it from the start, and everybody warned me. How could I have been so stupid? Twice.

Why would he gift me his house, though? Guilt? Because it was bad enough that he was going to rip my heart out, he felt bad about taking my business too? Or did he not plan to go back to her, but when she turned up he just couldn't resist her? The thoughts swirl around my mind until I'm dizzy with them.

I step out of the shower and boil the kettle for tea out of habit. Every single movement is an effort. Even the six-foot walk from the dressing table to the bed seems like a lengthy one. I want to crawl under the covers and hide forever. The shame is nothing compared to the gaping hurt inside. Flopping back onto the mattress in my towelling robe, I sip on the scalding tea. Even the physical pain fails to distracts me from the emotional one.

I flip my phone over in my hand out of habit. I'm not expecting to hear from him. Or anyone else. The party was in full swing when I left. There will be more than a few sore heads this morning. If I don't surface until the afternoon, I'm pretty sure no one will notice.

An *Ireland Today* news alert pops up, informing me that Ireland's favourite hooker is about to become a father for the first time. A further horror inches into my gut, and a flash-back of his fingers on her stomach in the bar winds me. I lurch up, tucking my feet under me again and open the full article.

Maria Vaillancourt has announced on her social media pages this morning that she is expecting her first baby with boyfriend, Eddie Harrington, Ireland's rugby hooker. The French tennis player reports that it's early days, but she and the baby are both doing well. Maria claims Eddie is over the moon with the news and is expected to make a full statement on his return from Croatia, where he is attending former teammate, Callum Connolly's wedding to Irish Radio presenter, Abby Queenan.

Will it be a bouncing baby boy? Or a beautiful baby girl? Either way, that child has sport in their veins, and we can't wait to see what glory he or she will bring our country in the future.

My worst fears are confirmed. I barely make it to the toilet bowl before I throw up the tea.

CHAPTER THIRTY-THREE

EDDIE

The hurt on Emma's face is unbearable. I feel every single sliver of her agony, every pang of passing pain because it replicates my own. I had to get Maria out before she created one of her spectacular dramatic scenes. I couldn't risk her ruining Callum and Abby's big day or saying something to Emma that I wouldn't be able to take back. Although from the look on her face, the damage is irreparable anyway. Nausea twists in my guts, but I continue guiding Maria out of the bar and as far away from here as physically possible.

If she is carrying my child, I can't take the chance she might walk out of here and consider aborting it. That would sit on my conscience forever. Family is the most important thing in the world to me. I just hadn't planned on having one with her. Jesus, I've only slept with two women the entire year, yet I managed to get the wrong one pregnant. Even though it's been less than a week, I already know deep down that if Emma was carrying my child, I wouldn't feel a hint of the horror that I'm holding now. Clearly, I haven't lost my knack of fucking up everything I touch.

Taking deep, even breaths to steady my emotions, I guide her through reception, hunching down my six-foot-two frame in the hope that I don't meet any more wedding guests.

'My rental is outside. I booked into a boutique hotel in the old town. Will you come back with me?'

The second I've guided her out of the hotel, I yank my hand away from her back.

'I will, but not in the circumstances you might be hoping for.'

I can't lie to her, I can't tell her everything will be fine, that I'll take care of her, because I can't make that promise. Knowing my family values, she probably assumes I'll marry her. I don't think I can...not now...not ever. Even though it might be what my own family would expect.

'Eddie...this isn't what we planned, but I can't help *vinking* it might be fate.'

She presses the fob, and lights flash on a red convertible as it unlocks. I follow her across the carpark. Noel is out having another sneaky cigar. He raises his eyebrows but says nothing.

I drop into the passenger side as she starts the engine. I won't have this conversation with Maria until she is safely back in her hotel room, and I have taken the car keys from her. With her temper, she is liable to do anything. As much as I don't want her in my life, I won't risk her doing anything erratic while carrying my child. I bite my tongue and bide my time.

The tarmac is smooth beneath the wheels, but the street lighting leaves a lot to be desired. The luminous moon and multiple twinkling stars are the only sources of light. Maria flicks on the full beam, cruising at seventy kilometres an hour along the coast road. The inbuilt navigation system interjects occasionally, otherwise, it's silent.

The Adriatic Sea is to my right, as the cliff drops over two hundred metres. I remember how any time we've taken this road, Emma can't even look. For a woman with her ruthless reputation, she certainly has a lot of irrational fears, heights being right up there at the top. Maria, on the other hand, is reckless.

'Slow down, Maria. There are some sharp bends ahead.'

'It's a lot to take in,' she says, placing a hand on my thigh. It sends a frisson of dread through me, and not just because I'd rather she left it on the steering wheel.

'It is.' I deliberately try not to get drawn in yet.

Three minutes pass in silence, the atmosphere growing heavier with every second. I contemplate the possibility that she might have been so calculating as to do this deliberately, to trap me into a situation where she knows I'll feel obliged to play a role. Even if it's not the role she wants.

I count back the dates, mentally trying to determine when this could possibly have happened. I haven't slept with her in eight weeks. The summer had been crazy with her new tennis academy, and I only made it to Paris twice between training and matches.

'Say *somewing*, Eddie, for god's sake.' She turns her head to squint at me through the dark.

'Eyes on the road, Maria, for fuck's sake.'

'Don't swear at me, Eddie, I'm your girlfriend, not one of your teammates.'

If she is, it's news to me. I tut loudly, my patience is wearing thin. It's a struggle to keep my mouth shut. I purse my lips firmly together, eyes squinting through the darkness at the winding road ahead.

She lets out an exaggerated dramatic sigh. It's probably killing her that she can't coax me into an argument, invoke some sort of reaction from me. Oh, she will get one as soon as she is safely back in her hotel room. It just won't be the reaction she's hoping for.

'Eddie, talk to me. I've just told you I'm pregnant, and you're sitting there like a fucking mute.'

She twists her head again as we round one of the more dangerous bends. Her eyes are averted from the road for a fraction of a second. It's a fraction too long. Bright light blinds me. I look up, hearing the bang a split second before feeling the effect of it. Apparently lightning really does strike twice.

CHAPTER THIRTY-FOUR

EMMA

Karen, Fran and Kerry gather in the humungous bed around me. Ruffled sheets are strewn aside as they squish in next to me in support. If I was in any doubt of what a wreck I am, it's mirrored in the sympathy etched on their faces. They're still unused to seeing me without my usual cosmetic armour on. I've been hiding behind a painted face since we were about fifteen, back in the days where the nuns used to threaten us with five hundred verses of the rosary for talking in class.

They came knocking about an hour ago. In a rare serious moment, Marcus apparently pulled Karen aside and told her I might need a friend this morning. He wasn't wrong. Perhaps Abby was right, maybe there *is* a heart of gold hiding underneath that hairy, loud exterior.

'Maybe they got it wrong?' Karen says, placing a gentle hand protectively on my back.

'I doubt it. There's no such thing as smoke without fire, and let's face it, he had been having sex with her.' A fresh wave of hurt and anger reverberates through me.

'Even if she is pregnant, they broke up. Eddie wants you. This is the twenty-first century. There is nothing stating that he has to marry her,' Kerry says.

I haven't forgotten what I saw between her and Nathan last night. I wonder has she? I have no intention of bringing it up either way, I've got bigger problems now anyway.

'He picked her. He doesn't want me. Besides, family is everything to him, he told me himself.' I wrap my arms around my chest. Eddie and I are over.

'Maybe you should at least try and talk to him, Emma. He gifted you his house, for goodness sake. Men don't do that. Okay, I appreciate he can probably afford it, but it was his shelter, his own private space. His way of saying he's willing to give you everything. I can't imagine he invited Maria here.'

I'm certain he didn't invite her, but it doesn't change his actions when she arrived. I can't shake the disappointment that's squeezing my chest. The enormity of what I've lost, how close I came (even if it was only in my mind) to having it all.

There's no way he's not going to stand by Maria, and I'd never dream of asking him otherwise. Eddie loves kids. He can't wait to be a dad, he told me so himself. I have to accept it's truly finished this time.

As soon as I'm physically able to pull myself together, to finish mourning the life I almost had, I'll sign his house back over. It will be the perfect place to raise a family, he'll see that now. I'll find somewhere of my own to launch my new salon, channel all of my time and effort back to my business as I originally planned – a plan that I will never waver from. My energy will blow fire into everything I touch, and I will never allow myself to get hurt again.

'Girls. Can I ask you a massive favour?' I need them to do something for me.

'Anything.' Kerry takes my hand and squeezes it. Fran

nods from across the room, where she is loading a capsule into the coffee machine. She really has become one of us, and it's only now I've come to appreciate the quiet calm that she radiates.

'It's the second last day of our holiday. Can we please get absolutely rip-roaring drunk and chalk this whole thing with Eddie up to experience. We need to make sure Abby enjoys the last few days of her wedding. I'm going to need copious amounts of alcohol, regular hugs and an endless supply of laughter to help me put on a brave face.'

Even then, I'm not sure I'll survive it, but their pity is tearing me apart.

'That, my friend, is something I'm an expert at.' Kerry pipes up with a glint in her eyes. Huh, I know too well, but I still don't mention it. Fran and Karen share a glance which basically translates as an acknowledgement they're likely to be babysitting grown-ups for the day. Karen shrugs, and Fran nods.

'Go and put your face on. Let's get this show on the road.' Karen knows me all too well. Though today, I've had enough of painting on the mask. If I'm honest, it has never done me any favours, other than attract all the wrong men and add pressure to pretend I'm naturally flawless. In truth, we are all fucking flawed, whether it be on the inside, on the outside, or usually both.

Today, I am ready to accept mine. I am what I am. Although it wasn't enough to secure me the man of my dreams, he saw me and seemed to accept me as I am. It wasn't enough in the end, it's about time I accepted myself this way, imperfections and all.

'I'm going like this.' I gesture to my naked face, and the girls stare at me open-mouthed.

'What? It's not like I'm trying to impress anyone.' And for the first time since I was a teenager, it's the truth.

CHAPTER THIRTY-FIVE

EDDIE

Something scratches against my left arm, irritating me to the point that it's all I'm aware of. I reach up with my right hand to swat it away, but it's stuck, attached to my skin. My eyes fly open in alarm.

An unfamiliar face looks down on me. 'Stay still. Everything is going to be okay,' a heavy man in a paramedic's uniform informs me.

I blink twice, moving my lips to speak, but only a muffled sound comes out. The panic sets in for a split second until I realise I'm wearing an oxygen mask. I lift my hand up to move it, but the paramedic holds it firmly in position.

'Rest. Everything is going to be okay. Your girlfriend is fine. She's in the ambulance in front, just a few scratches. You were both very lucky.'

———

On the ward, a young female doctor examines me. She removes a slim torch from the pocket of her navy scrubs and shines it into my right eye, then my left, before switching it off with a pronounced click and dropping it back into her pocket.

'How do you feel?'

'My head is sore.' My fingers trace the stitches on my left temple, another scar to add to my rapidly increasing collection of war wounds.

'Miraculously, your MRI came back clear.'

'How is Maria?'

'She has a few cuts, but you were both fortunate.'

I can barely bring myself to ask, but I have to know. I might not have chosen to have a baby with Maria, but I wouldn't choose to lose one if it was already there.

'And the baby?'

'What baby?'

'Maria is pregnant.'

The doctor looks down at her notes quizzically and back to me. Something is amiss, but what I don't know. Could she have lost the baby in the crash?

'Did you scan her? Is the baby okay?' The urgent tone of my voice seems to alarm her, and she takes a step back from the hospital bed that tightly tucked sheets bind me to.

'I can't discuss another patient's medical history with you I'm afraid. Patient confidentiality. Rest for a few hours, and I'll organise the paperwork for you to be released this afternoon.' She turns on her heels, but I leap forward and catch her by the arm.

'Please.' My voice is deliberately low, for all I know, Maria could be on the other side of the curtain. 'I fully understand the situation, but please, I implore you. Is the baby okay?'

The doctor places her pen back in her scrub pocket as she contemplates her response.

'The only reason I was in that car with Maria was because she told me she was having my baby. Do you understand me? I need to know, is the baby okay?'

One quizzically raised eyebrow hints that she has information that I need, but refuses to reveal it.

'I'm afraid I can't discuss this with you any further, Mr Harrington.'

As soon as she leaves, I yank the tubing from my arm and swing my legs off the side of the bed. I have to find Maria. I need to know if the baby is okay. The guilt is eating me alive. I didn't plan this baby, and for a split second last night, I wished it wasn't there, but I didn't mean for this to happen; I didn't mean for it to die. I can't cope with another ruined life on my conscience.

I scramble around the tiny pine bedside locker to locate my belongings. My phone is gone, lost in transit, my suit trousers are in a crumpled pile with my bloodstained shirt. My fingers instinctively go to my forehead, where I feel a small wound and the plastic wisps of stitches. I got off lightly. I'm like a cat with nine fucking lives. Someone up there seems to be looking out for me. It's more than I deserve.

I pull on the dishevelled clothes, aware that I could pass for a homeless person, and yank back the curtain to go in search of Maria. There are three other beds in this ward. The one directly opposite me contains a sleeping man in his eighties. The one to the right of me is empty. And the last one houses a boy who looks to be fifteen or so and barely glances up from his phone to acknowledge me.

My feet are unsteady beneath me, but desperation to find them spurs me on. I slip out into the main corridor, peering into the various wards leading off the main route. I'm almost at the end when I spot her, tucked into the corner of a ward, staring up at the ceiling.

'What are you doing?' a nurse asks me from behind as I

stare through the open doorway at the woman carrying my child. She's okay. She looks okay anyway.

'I'm with her.' I point at Maria, who glances round at the sound of my voice.

Four long strides position me at the side of her bed.

'Are you okay?'

'Yes. We were lucky.' She places a hand over her tummy protectively.

'And the baby?'

'Shhh, Eddie, keep it down.' She frowns at me, as the nurse approaches.

Shh? What does she mean shhh? Is the baby okay or not?

'Maria, did they do a scan? Is the baby okay?' I simply can't drop it. I need to know. Why won't she tell me?

The nurse stops what she is doing and blatantly stares at us like she's watching a tennis ball bounce back and forth.

Maria looks at the floor.

'Goddammit, Maria, is the baby okay?'

It dawns on me then, slowly, like the sun rising after the darkest night of my life. There is no baby. There never was.

It was a calculated ploy to ensnare me in an elaborate trap. A trap which I'd ran into, without question, blinded by guilt and the need to protect. My god, if I'd have been stupid enough to get back with her, to sleep with her again, she might have even fallen pregnant then and fiddled the dates.

Still, she says nothing. It's the first time I've ever known her to be silent.

'How could you lie to me?'

The nurse backs out of the room, scurrying back to the nurses' station.

'I'm sorry, Eddie. I love you. I wanted us to be together.'

She is crazy. Crazy and calculated. I have to get out of here.

'Stay away from me, Maria. I don't want to see you again.'

I run from the hospital, grateful to be freed from this short-term nightmare. Out on the street, I flag a taxi, simultaneously formulating a plan to fix things with Emma. She's always intuitively known I've held a bit of something back from her, a part of myself. She believed it was to do with Maria. After my departure last night, the only way I'll be able to prove otherwise is to tell her the real truth.

What a wake-up call. I'm not going to be tied to Maria with a child I didn't wish for but would undoubtedly have loved. It wasn't karma. It was a lie.

I need to start living. Stop hiding. Stop wallowing. Let it go. I'm no good to anyone half in the present, half stuck on my mistakes, but that is easier said than done. How can I remove this crippling, excuse the pun, demon from my shoulders? I can't think straight with him there. I can't just shake it off, still unworthy of forgiveness. I don't know how to get over it, to feel better.

Confess.

The thought pops into my head out of nowhere, and I'm catapulted back to my ten-year-old self, to my altar boy days beside Father Davy at St Mary's Cathedral. I can practically smell the incense, the smoke brushing the back of my throat. It knocks the wind from me like a forceful tackle from the toughest All Black.

Maybe if I confess everything I'll feel better? The trouble is, I haven't been to church since I was sixteen, and in all honesty, faith is something that has eluded me for my entire adult life. The thought of a god looking down, watching out for us, seems completely implausible when children are starving, innocent people are dying every second of the day, and so much of it down to some sort of weird battle over religion, over whose god is real. It is utter madness.

So who *could* I confess to, to make me feel better? Emma? Even if it means I risk losing everything?

There's a good chance she will run for the hills when she realises the damage that I'm capable of. Shit, I wouldn't even blame her. Will it absolve my guilt if I'm honest and pay the utmost price, losing her?

No, but it's a start. I bite my lower lip and consider my options.

A taxi pulls up, and I get in. The driver asks how I am, glancing at the fresh wound on my head. I don't tell him it's the ones we can't see that are the most painful.

Coach told me to keep quiet about what happened last year, said it would look bad on the team. But this whole Croatia trip looks bad, what with the video of our captain singing the national anthem naked, the team hooker hospitalised and considering blowing the whistle on the biggest secret of his life. I better ask Callum if there's room for one more in the commentators' box.

It's taken me a year to realise, and another near miss, but I think the only way to shake my demons is to come clean, admit my truth to her. Until I do, I can't escape it. If I'm going to let it go, I need to get it off my chest. Trust is fundamental to Emma. I need to be honest with her. We can't build a life on my lie. I have to do something, right my wrongs and accept responsibility for what I've done. Because it's seeping into every aspect of my life, and I can't think straight through the guilt and shame.

It's almost lunchtime by the time the taxi arrives at The Oceania hotel. I head gingerly into reception to get money to pay him, expecting to see someone I know mulling around the common areas. Though perhaps after last night's party, they are all nursing headaches, not a million miles away from my own. It's not just the crash, it's more like my head has been blown off my neck with the biggest epiphany of my life.

I'm in two minds if I should go straight to Emma's room, to find her, to explain, grovel and tell her everything. I lost my phone somewhere in transit. It's probably at the bottom of the ocean bed; maybe the sharks are watching YouTube on it. A quick glance down at myself reminds me I'm filthy, and my clothes are tattered. I head to my own room to freshen up first and take a double dose of the prescription painkillers from my luggage.

My room is on the third floor, not far from the one I accidentally disturbed after the casino stag night, with the tattooed Americans. That seems like a lifetime ago. It's been an eventful few days. I can't wait to get back on Irish soil.

As sunny and luxurious as it is here, I miss my own bed. Although technically I've given my bed up, and my house, for Emma. I could be doing with a few days to sort my meagre belongings out. The place is actually very well set up to be a chic spa, what with the calming minimal décor and plush carpets I settled on.

My thoughts are interrupted as I open the door of my immaculate suite. The shrill sound of ringing from the phone beside the bed echoes around the room.

'Hello?'

'Eddie, where have you been, man? Marcus said Maria was here, then there was no sign of either of you! I thought she'd boiled your bones for soup.'

'It was close. Sorry for the disruption. I hope it didn't impact your wedding night.' Desperate to change the subject and put it all behind me as one of the worst nights of my life, I revert back to my usual tactics. 'Did you consummate that marriage yet?'

'Ha. I certainly did, while you were busy chugging free champagne at the drinks reception. Oww. Sorry, honey.'

I snigger. 'I'll leave you to it, man. I need to find Emma.'

Abby says something to Callum in the background, but I can't quite make out what she's saying.

'Erm, Ed?' The tone of his voice has changed. My stomach twists into a niggle of worry.

'Did you see the Irish news today? Well, not the news technically. It's that daft gossip column that runs alongside it. Ava Armstrong's gig.' He pauses while I wonder if they got wind of my brush with death.

'I don't look at that bullshit, but even if I did, I've lost my phone. I didn't see a thing.'

'Don't shoot the messenger.' He hesitates, and a cold feeling drifts through my veins.

'What is it, Callum?'

'Is Maria pregnant?' he blurts.

'No, but that's exactly what she told me last night. It was a lie.'

How does he know?

'Well, she's been on the news telling everyone she's having your baby.'

'You have got to be fucking joking me.' She is fucking relentless.

The blood drains from my face, and not for the first time this day, I feel like I've been hit by an oncoming truck. I have no choice but to put a stop to this once and for all.

CHAPTER THIRTY-SIX

EMMA

We find four white plastic sunloungers on the beach. The thin mattress is hot beneath my stomach as I lie on my front, gazing out at the glistening turquoise sea. I've come to love this place. If I ever get over Eddie Harrington, I will definitely come back. Until then, it will have to remain locked in my memory until I can open it again without it ripping me apart.

Everywhere I look, I'm reminded of the time we spent together. On the horizon, I see the Elafiti Islands; at the pool, I see him pulling me under and lifting me on his shoulders; when I look at the sparkling waves of the sea, I remember wrapping my legs around his waist and giving myself to him for the second time.

He will be a hard man to get over.

'I thought we were getting rip-roaring drunk?' Kerry reminds us as Jacov heads towards us with a friendly smile. Maybe she does remember? Maybe she feels terrible inside and needs to blot out reality as much as I do. No, on second thoughts, she's always like this.

'It's midday,' Karen says, pushing her sunglasses up from where they are sliding down her nose in this clammy heat.

'Exactly. I'm parched. We'll start early, have a good old daytime drinking session and get into bed early, fresh for tomorrow's travels.' Kerry sits up and smiles meaningfully at Jacov. She needn't have bothered. He's worked out exactly who will be waiting for him in the short few days we've been here.

Karen shrugs, accepting her fate as Kerry orders a pitcher of Sex On The Beach. As far as fate goes, drinking pitchers of luminous coloured cocktails on a Croatian beach isn't exactly a hardship.

And it really is the last hoo-hah – our final full day here.

Abby spots us from the pool and walks the length of the stone-paved pathway to the beach. She wears a white strappy cotton dress and supports the baby on her right hip. Abby is the walking advert for married life: glowing skin, bright eyes, and her smile could illuminate the Eiffel Tower.

'Here's Mrs Connolly,' Karen says, and we offer a collective cheer.

'What a fantastic day, Abs. Thank you for letting us be a part of it.' Kerry stands and throws her arms around Abby and Casey.

'Girls, I couldn't imagine doing it without you. Such an effort you all made to be here. Thank you. It was honestly the best day of my life.' She deliberately doesn't mention Eddie's absence. I have no idea if she knows.

'Sit down.' I stand from my position and offer her my lounger. 'We'll get another bed.'

'I'd love to, but I can't. I have to get around all the relations before they start leaving, and my mother loses her shit completely because I didn't spend enough time with them. Will you come up to the pool for the BBQ later?'

'Of course.' I picture seeing Eddie and my stomach lurches. Will he arrive with Maria? His loyalty is elsewhere now.

'Walk with me for a minute, Em.'

I stand, rub Casey's rosy little cheek and step into line beside Abby, strolling towards the sea. The warm ocean foam sprays up over my toes before pulling back again, leaving me dry. It seems to sum up my current situation precisely.

'I'm so sorry about Eddie.'

I draw in a long deep breath and hold it into my lungs for as long as I can, until it wooshes out in an almighty sigh and I admit one of my deepest darkest secrets out loud. There has to be some benefit to being friends with Ireland's most successful agony aunt.

'It's okay. If my own mother can't love me, how can I expect a man to, especially one like Eddie? Jesus, I'm getting ahead of myself with the L-word, I meant hypothetically speaking.' I scrape my fingers through my hair and re-tie it into a loose ponytail.

'Is that what you think, Emma? That your mother doesn't love you?' Abby leans forward and takes my hand, her features regrouping into a concerned frown.

'I know she doesn't. I don't actually know if she knows the meaning of the word. She goes easier on Grace because she's married and because she's is growing the first grandchild blissfully in her womb. Holly's the baby of the family, so that seems to give her some kind of leeway. Me, I've always been kind of insignificant, no matter what I've achieved.'

I didn't mean to say it out loud, any of it, but it's the truth. Before tonight, I never realised how much my mother's disapproval affected me and probably influenced my constant quest for love.

'Don't ever think you are insignificant. You are one of the most driven, ambitious, successful women I have ever had the pleasure of meeting, let alone calling my friend. Your mother's issues lie with her, not you. I don't think there's anything you could have said or done differently throughout your life that could have made her warmer towards you. Was she always this way?'

'She got worse when Dad started working abroad. When he left, it was like she could barely look at me or something.'

Abby lets out a tut and strokes the back of my hand.

'Want to know what I think? I don't want to force my opinions on you or anything, but I do sort of do this stuff for a living...' Her lip curls into a wry smile.

'Shoot. Then I don't want to talk about it again.'

'I've only met your father once, Christmas last year, when he called into the salon, but something struck me then, and I think it might have something to do with why your mum keeps you at arm's length.'

She has my attention now because I have spent years pondering precisely that.

'Did it ever occur to you that you are the absolute image of your father? Both of your sisters are fairer than you, blue-eyed, like your mother. You, on the other hand, have your father's dark hair, his eye colouring, and you even inherited his drive for business. I don't actually think it's you that your mother is rejecting. I think it's your father.'

'Wow. That is deep.' I swallow hard and consider her words. Whether she's right or wrong, something strikes a chord, providing a tiny bit of comfort.

'Think about it. You are like him in almost every way. It's easier to relate to Grace because they have more in common.'

'Thank you.' I squeeze her hand back. She's certainly given me food for thought.

'Don't put yourself down. Eddie would be lucky to have

you. Any man would be. Maybe you should talk to him? Half the problems in this world would be solved if people would just talk honestly.'

'Jesus, Abs, you should be an advert for a mobile phone company or something with that line.' We giggle together, lightening the mood for a second before I remember the true crux of the problem.

'It doesn't change the fact that she's having his baby.'

'According to Callum, she's not.'

'What?' It comes out as a high-pitched squeak.

'Look, it's not my place to say, but it's complicated. Eddie thinks she might be lying, but it's her word at the minute. It seems a little too convenient, doesn't it? Eddie told Callum there was some sort of accident.'

'An accident? Is he okay?'

'Yes, it was minor. They were very lucky. He escaped with a few stitches.'

It didn't occur to me that something might have happened to him again. I simply thought he'd seen Maria once again and rejected me. I expected it almost. Maybe if I'd been more direct last year, instead of following my unwritten dating rules, he might have realised how much I cared and consequently not run off with a woman who makes no qualms about displaying her emotions for him publicly, be them good or bad.

'Anyway, it is what it is now. There's not a lot I can do about it. He has more than just her to think about now.'

'I wouldn't bet on it, but we can't rule it out yet.' Abby shoots a sympathetic glance in my direction, but I deliberately look away. We can overanalyse everything another time. Today, it's simply not appropriate. We walk across the warm sand back to the girls.

'We'll be up in a little while,' Karen tells her, not wishing to dwell on the wreckage.

'Okay, I'll see you girls in a bit.' She sashays away with a wave, the baby lifts her hand too. She's so adorable, it would make any woman broody. But for now, I'll just have to accept the only baby I'm going to have any time soon is my business.

Later in the afternoon, we head up to the barbecue as promised. The cocktails, the comforting company of my friends and the brilliant sunshine are not enough to soothe my fragile heart. People are talking about me, and I'm not the paranoid type. I can only assume they've read the same article as me, they've heard the pregnancy rumours and assumed I was either stupid enough not to know, or cruel enough not to care.

Sitting with the girls by the poolside, I do my best to keep a low profile, consoling myself that I will soon be home, back doing what I do best – working. At least nobody can take that from me. I have a lot of work to do finding new premises, and for the first time since I heard I'd lost the auction, I am actually pleased, because finding new premises will give me something to focus on.

Karen's phone chimes with a message. 'Shitting hell, girls, have you seen this latest update?'

She passes me her phone. A picture of Eddie and me on the boat trip sits adjacent to a new article. That turncoat Donal! I read on, only beginning to appreciate the extent of the damage.

Emotionless Eddie cheats on pregnant girlfriend.

It has emerged only hours after Maria's earlier pregnancy announcement that Eddie Harrington, Irish rugby legend and first-time, father-to-be, has been continuing a secret affair with Dublin-based beauty business tycoon Emma Harvey. While Eddie's pregnant girlfriend nursed her morning sickness, they continued an illicit relationship in the sunshine, at mutual friends' Callum and Abby Connolly's Dubrovnik wedding.

So far, Maria has refused to comment on the photo, and Mr

Harrington is currently unobtainable. Fans are beyond curious to see how this one plays out.

The comments are flying in beneath the article already:

Cheating scum.

They are all the same, more fool the women that get involved with them.

Home-wrecking whore.

Wonder would they consider a threesome.

Fuck. Who will want to go to a spa owned by a 'home-wrecking whore?' So much for nobody taking my businesses from me.

CHAPTER THIRTY-SEVEN

EDDIE

I'm waiting for my taxi to the airport when Noel arrives in the carpark. He's making the rounds, thanking his daughter's guests for coming and shaking everyone's hands.

'Did you ever get thrown that bone, son?' He claps me on the back with a strong warm hand and looks at me earnestly. Why is he asking? He saw me with Maria. He knows I managed to fuck everything up, like I always do.

'I did. It was the juiciest bone I ever had.' I offer Noel a wry smile.

'Want to talk about it?' He pulls his trousers at the knee to give a little wiggle room, in a manner that I've seen my own father do a hundred times.

'There's not a lot to say except that everything I touch seems to break. Even something as strong as a bone.'

'That's the thing about bones, they are partial to the odd break. But they do eventually heal.' He taps the side of his nose, like he's letting me in on the secrets of the world.

'What if it's like an old injury, that you break for the

second time, then all of a sudden you're out the game for good?' I recognise the low desperation in my voice and hate myself for it, amongst other things.

'Even the worst breaks heal. Of course they heal easier if you take the weight off them.' Noel nods, his vacant eyes mist as though he's referring to something else entirely. Something way more personal.

A flash of the pained look on Emma's face haunts me.

'You're not the only one with scars, Eddie. Callum told me what happened. Both with Emma and your brother. I hope you don't mind. It certainly won't go any further. But I need to tell you something. Don't spend the rest of your life thinking you deserve every bad thing that happens to you. You don't.'

'How do you know?'

'You're a good kid. I've seen enough of you boys over the last year to make a call on it.'

'You heard about Maria?'

'I did. Is it true?'

'No, but I can't prove it, and she's shouting it all over the media, and there's nothing I can do about it.'

Noel's lips purse into a wistful grimace. 'Son, you might not be able to stop her shouting about it, but you can shout louder. Play her at her own game. You have an entire PR team at your disposal. Use them.'

'It's not just that. It's one thing after another. I seem to tarnish everything I touch. Did Callum tell you about the house?'

'Yes. It was a crazy coincidence, that's all. You and Emma aren't doomed. Not if you don't want to be. Love is like every other game in life – you have to work at it. There are times where Cathy Queenan and I have almost broken along the way. Over bigger stuff than a house and a phantom baby. If you want Emma, stick with her. If anything, your behaviour has been pretty honourable; attempting to stand by a woman who claimed to be carrying your child, buying a property for your brother. You're a good lad. She'll see that.'

Noel stands, patting me on the back again and heads back inside.

His words swirl around my aching brain.

I always jump to the conclusion that bad things that happen are owed to me. That I not only deserve them but attract them each time I dare to chance happiness. Everything stems back to Matthew's accident. I assume that the universe wants to punish me because subconsciously, I feel like that's what I deserve because of what I've done.

Maybe, instead of accepting the negative things in my life, I should work on fixing them? Fix things with Emma. She is the best thing that ever happened to me, yet twice I've let her go because I felt I don't deserve her. It's about time I started fighting *for* her.

I've had enough. I'm done being the underdog. I will do everything in my power to become the man that does deserve her. I'm going to make this right. I'm going to banish my demons for good, but for now, I'll start by clearing up the rumours surrounding Maria. The only way I can do that is to head directly to the source, walk unarmed into the lion's lair.

CHAPTER THIRTY-EIGHT

EMMA

I'm dreaming again, that same haunting recurring dream. My heart hammers within my chest, and my hands automatically wrap around myself protectively. I'm running the length of the beach barefoot, broken shells slice the soles of my feet, but the pain doesn't stop me. The sky's black overhead, a heaviness threatens from above, the air pressurised, waiting for the release that only the most violent of thunderstorms can offer.

I'm searching for someone again. The same person I've been looking for in all of my dreams. The only difference is, this time, I know who it is – Eddie.

His broad silhouette is barely visible in the distance, moving continuously. I can't keep up. Sweat pours from me as I try. A flash of lightning strikes the ground between us, and an almighty rumble from the sky rattles around my ears. And with the second flash of lightning, he is gone.

The tears roll freely across my cheeks as I realise my

subconscious has pretty much summed up the situation perfectly. And it has nothing to do with maintaining a reputable business.

CHAPTER THIRTY-NINE

EDDIE

It's not exactly the homecoming I'd planned. Keira waits at Dublin airport for me, insisting we talk the second I land. I make my way through passport control once again.

At almost ten p.m., the sun has set, but the sky is still a brilliant pink, providing enough light to spot my sister standing outside the terminal building, an oversized scarf wrapped around her shoulders, a cigarette pinched between her index finger and her thumb. Things must be worse than I imagined, because she hasn't smoked since she had the kids five years ago.

'Eddie.' She stubs out her cigarette, her brown eyes narrowing as she glances around, suspicious of any hiding paparazzi. I was never particularly interesting to the media until I hooked up with Maria. She's an international tennis champion. I'm merely one of a large team, a team that I can often hide behind.

'How are you, sis?'

She doesn't reply as she ushers me into her burgundy

Kodiak, which is illegally parked in the drop off zone and covered in discarded rice cake wrappers and empty boxes of Peppa Pig raisins.

'Jesus, Eddie, this whole thing is such a mess. Mam is heartbroken. Dad is adamant that you'll have to marry her. Amy's upset because the one time we met Maria, we thought she was an ignorant bitch. Sorry, I shouldn't have blurted that out, but it's true. If you misbehave now, you'll lose your sponsorship deals, your career will suffer as the media tear their claws through you. I'm worried about you.'

'Relax, will you?' I hadn't considered my parents in all of this. I need to put them out of their misery immediately. 'There is no baby,' I tell her as she puts the car into first gear, pulling away from several ogling faces peering in the window.

'Thank god, Eddie. Oh my god, I've been worried sick. Do you know what she's calling you? Emotionless Eddie.'

I try not to laugh. Emotionless Eddie is filled with emotion, just none relating to Maria. It's not funny, truly, but if I don't laugh, I might actually cry. How's that for emotion?

'What happened to your head?' She glances sideways at me as she curls around the narrow one-way system to the valet park.

'I was in a car accident. Last night.'

'Fuck. It's almost a year to the day since your last one. That's kind of creepy. Are you okay?' She squints at me again.

'Fine, but keep your eyes on the road; I don't want to be in another.'

'Talk to me, Eddie. How are we going to handle this? Do you want me to make a statement, or will the team PR handle this?'

I take a deep breath and exhale slowly, steaming up the windscreen in front of me. I've had an idea, but I'm fifty-fifty on whether I have the balls to go through with it. It's possibly the only way I can achieve a modicum of inner peace, by letting it all off.

'I'm thinking of going public.'

'About Emma? She does not look good in all of this. The press will crucify both of you. I can see the headlines now: 'Emotionless Eddie abandons pregnant girlfriend for beautician.'

'Maria is not pregnant,' I remind her. 'And Emma is not your average beautician. She has four, almost five businesses. She's the most ambitious woman I've ever met. Not to mention, funny, kind and strong.' I don't add that she's the one I've thought of continuously for the past year, and the one I keep letting slip through my fingers.

Keira's mobile pings from the centre console. She picks it up, scanning and scrolling like a mad woman, before taking out another cigarette.

'I thought you had problems before. Check this out.' She throws the phone into my lap and lights her cigarette with shaky fingers.

I look at the article on her phone. It's written by the same columnist as this morning's breaking news, Ava Armstrong, but it's the picture beneath that's the real problem. A photo of me and Emma on Bob's boat stares back at me. My arms are wrapped around her, leaning in to kiss her neck, eyes captured staring down at her chest. I barely recognise myself. Apart from looking like a total love rat, I actually look happy, free, alive and practically youthful again. It must have been taken by that redhead Donal or the girlfriend. Fuck.

Whatever about me, I can't have them talking about Emma like that. Shit, this will ruin her and her business.

I can't let that happen.

'I need to make a phone call.'

CHAPTER FORTY

EMMA

The buzzing of my mobile wakes me from my disturbed alcohol-induced slumber. I pat the side of the bed until I find it. A crushing weight bears down on my chest. My dream is so fresh, so raw; it feels real.

'Hello?' My voice is gritty, my mouth dry. By eleven p.m., I'd ended up at an eight on the Kerry-O'Metre, and Karen had thankfully walked me to my room. I'd needed the Dutch courage to get through the BBQ with the main topic of conversation centring around the latest online article, labelling me as Ireland's biggest homewrecker.

I'd read a few of the comments that came tearing in underneath the article, none of them particularly flattering.

However hurtful they might be, however damaging to my business, what still hurts the most is the thought that *his* baby might be growing inside another woman's womb. Jealousy is a horrendous, all-consuming emotion, and it's wreathing, wriggling and quadrupling inside of me.

'Em?' Karen checks I'm still with her. I can't say much

because I'm dangerously close to breaking into a complete wailing ball of emotion, yet again.

'You have to get online. Eddie is apparently going on *Ireland This Morning* with that battle-axe Ava Armstrong,' Karen shrieks, and I wince as her voice whistles through my eardrum.

I scramble up into a seating position. 'You have got to be fucking kidding?' Eddie hates the media, hates the celebrity bullshit, and most of all hates Ava Armstrong.

'Shall we come over?' Karen offers.

'Yes. Please. I warn you I'm a fucking wreck, though.'

'Believe it or not, Emma, it's allowed. See you in five.'

I yank my iPad from my suitcase, where everything is packed by the door, ready to leave.

A fresh wave of bubbling, churning anxiety eats at the lining of my stomach. Why is Eddie going on Ava Armstrong's show when she completely slated him, and me for that matter? He hates the media. I pray to god he's not going to cause a scene because it will only make things worse. When it comes to the media, you simply can't win. They have too much power. It's best to weather the storm.

CHAPTER FORTY-ONE

EDDIE

Ava Armstrong is one of the most ruthless women I've ever had the misfortune to come across. She is the female equivalent of a human sniffer dog, equipped with narrow eyes, a nose for trouble, and an uncanny ability to track her prey. And that is why I am about to reveal everything to her.

I sit on the red leather couch of the *Ireland This Morning* studio, with seven cameras pointing in my direction from multiple angles, awaiting my judgement. The studio is ridiculously bright. A young girl dabs a make-up brush on my face, but I turn my head away in a silent declination. One thing's for sure, I didn't come here to look good, quite the opposite in fact. I'm mentally exhausted from carrying around my guilt, my secrets, my shame. I'm done hiding the truth, pretending I'm something I'm not. It's been eating me alive, and hopefully, my confession will provide more of a story than the one that's currently causing Emma a phenomenal amount of damage. If it costs me my place on the team, then so be it.

Keira and Amy sit in the fake live audience. Amy chews her nails, Keira taps her foot impatiently. She pleaded with me not to do this, promised me nobody need know. But I know. And I need to get it off my chest. While I'm already Ireland's most hated male, I'm as well to get all the damage done in one go. If it salvages Emma's reputation, it will be worth it.

Maria has gone oddly quiet, not even a post on Instagram or Twitter. She must have seen the newspaper picture of Emma and me. I have Callum's 'fixer' Declan currently obtaining proof of Maria's non-existent medical condition. It might not be strictly legal, but it's necessary to have in my possession to put a stop to the rumours once and for all.

Ava struts across the studio wearing skin-tight leather leggings and a cream blazer. She flashes me a smile that doesn't meet her eyes.

'Thank you for joining me today, Eddie. I can honestly say I didn't expect it, after everything.'

'You mean after you ran a story about me that was completely unfounded.' I sit up straighter in my seat.

'Are you referring to the one where your girlfriend is pregnant? Or the one where you're looking a little bit too cosy with your *other* girlfriend?' Her razor-sharp tongue is notorious, but her words can't torture me any more than my own silence has.

'Let's save the chat for the camera, shall we?' I don't want to give her any ammunition or inkling as to where this is going.

We don't have to wait long.

The cameraman counts down, signalling five, four, three, two, one, with his nicotine-stained fingers, and I brace myself for the biggest defeat of my life.

CHAPTER FORTY-TWO

EMMA

I'm wedged between Karen and Fran in my hotel bed once again, with Kerry lying widthways across the bottom.

'Quick! It's starting!' Karen says, and Kerry leaps up to squash in behind us, four sets of eyes trained on a ten-inch, quivering screen.

'Here, I'll hold it,' Fran offers, the calmest out of the lot of us as usual.

The familiar bars of the theme music sound and my nerves are shot to pieces.

The camera focuses only on Ava, we don't yet see who her guests are. Shit, it could all be rumours. Eddie might not even be there.

'Good morning, thank you for joining us today on *Ireland This Morning*. Today we have a special guest with us to discuss *those* rumours we've all been talking about, followed by Instagram sensation Stella Holmes with some beauty blogging advice. Ireland's very own M.O.D.E.R.N will be here in the studio later with some live music, having recently returned from the States to kick off their first world tour.'

She's scarily good in front of the camera; poised, elegant and sharp. Her make-up is immaculate, and not a strand of her severe, bobbed hair even dares fall out of place.

'So let's welcome our first guest, Eddie Harrington, Ireland's very own rugby hooker, excuse the pun...' she snorts a little sarcastic laugh at her own joke.

The camera angle widens, showing Eddie sitting back in what is supposed to look like a relaxed position on the red leather couch, but I can tell he's troubled from the way he runs his thumb under his chin.

'Ava, thanks for having me on. It was a sensational article that you wrote about me. It's just a shame that it was a rumour and completely unfounded.'

Ava clicks her bony neck and rolls her eyes for the benefit of the camera, and all of the women of the country watching who have already condemned him to a slow and painful death before they've even heard his side of the story.

'We had a statement issued from Maria herself, which clearly stated—'

He clears his throat, sits forward and rudely interrupts his host.

'Really? Well, that's more than I had. There is no baby, but I'm simply a man, so I can't officially prove that yet. Maria's refusing to take my phone calls, and that was before you printed the picture of myself and Emma Harvey on holiday.'

I gasp. No baby. Could it really be true? I hadn't dared to believe Abby yesterday for fear of another epic disappointment. Karen and Kerry nudge me, but none of us utters a word, frightened we might miss something.

Eddie's tone is cool and even, but his jaw twitches. I can only imagine his insides must be alight with anger inside. I barely recognise this serious man, who never once inter-rupted me while I was talking. Though it doesn't change the facts, he still chose Maria over me. That is something that I'm still not sure I can get over.

'Ah, now we are getting somewhere.' A ruthless glint sparks in Ava's eyes, and she straightens her back in antic-ipation.

'I'm sure you are aware of a certain Twitter storm last Saturday, which resulted in Maria publicly dumping me. Nobody could have missed her blowing up another huge tantrum online. Again. Labelling me 'Emotionless Eddie.' I came here today to tell you that I am far from emotionless.'

'It's easy for someone like you to comment on emotions—'

'You know nothing about "someone like me". And that's exactly why I'm here. I come from a family of four children. I have seven nieces and nephews. I love children. I can't wait to be a father one day. Would I choose Maria as the mother of my children, given a choice? Honestly, no, I wouldn't.' He shakes his head, lowering his eyes from the camera for the first time.

'But you were happy enough to sleep with her. To call her your girlfriend.' Ava twists the knife in, daring him to chal-lenge her statement.

'I was not in a good place when I met Maria at the Italian Open. I was battling my own demons. It never should have gone further than that night. It was never serious. We are not compatible. We never were.'

My chest constricts, and I can barely breathe as he alludes to his big secret. The one where he wrongly feels responsible for his brother's car crash. Will he say it? My fingers grip Karen's, knuckles whitening in apprehension. He doesn't need to do this, to tell everyone. It wasn't his fault.

Ava rolls her eyes dramatically at the camera again, her

perfectly plucked eyebrows disappear beneath a sweeping side fringe. 'Missed a try or something, did you?' She sneers.

'I was in a car accident with my brother. We were hit sideways by a skidding lorry. It sliced the bonnet clean off the car.' He swallows hard as he recalls it.

'Oh.' Ava looks momentarily baffled. She glances down at her notepad in front of her, silently scanning for a mention of this, but of course, it's nowhere. This new information seems to throw her a bit as she crosses her legs and tries to assemble an appropriate answer.

'It wasn't in the papers,' she concludes.

'I paid a lot of money for it not to be. The accident left my brother Matthew paralysed from the waist down. He is in a wheelchair; he may never walk again.'

I pull the covers higher up around me as I wait for Ava to tear him to shreds on national television. Karen's fingers squeeze mine in silent support, none of us say a word. To anyone on the outside, it risks looking like he is using the 'my brother is in a wheelchair' card for sympathy.

'So you were involved in this accident when, exactly?' Ava's elongated nose scrunches into a distasteful sneer, still not entirely convinced of the relevancy of the incident.

'Last September, in the States.' Eddie's brown eyes gaze thoughtfully past the camera, as if he's not even seeing them, as if they are not even relevant.

'But you were still in a bad place in May when you met Maria?' Ava is trying to chip away the relevance of Eddie's story

'Because I was eaten alive by guilt and shame.' His eyes retrain on Ava. He seems to be checking she is following what he is saying before he delivers his punchline. That it was him, that Matthew was collecting from the airport. But he says the unspeakable. Something I never even considered. Yet it makes perfect sense.

'Everyone assumed Matthew was driving that day because it was his car. But it was me. I put him in that wheelchair.'

A shooting sense of clarity tears through me. How could I have not known? How did I not guess? That's why he had to have the property for Matthew. That's why making Matthew happy was more important than anything else in the world, even more important than his own happiness.

A sharp hiss of a gasp slips from Ava's tongue as she realises she's getting a major scoop, a story that's not yet been told.

'Did you know?' Karen asks from behind me.

'No. But now everything makes sense. I knew he was hiding something, but I thought it was something to do with her.' My eyes stay trained on the iPad, desperately waiting to see how his confession will be taken.

'Wow, Eddie. That is certainly a heavy cross to bear.' Ava's tone has switched to one harbouring slightly more sincerity than her previous one.

'I was adhering to the speed limit. My blood work showed no alcohol in my system, but if I'm totally honest – I was tired. Tired from the flight, tired from the night before. I can't help but wonder if I'd have been quicker with my responses or maybe more focused.'

'How is your brother Matthew now?'

'He's in surprisingly good form. His wife is an angel in disguise and his children keep him busy. He's actually moving home next month. I bought him a house, five doors down from mine. I've ordered the stairlift, and I'm making sure it's wheelchair friendly, though my sister Amy assures me she will have Matthew walking again. She's a physiotherapist, special-ising in rehabilitation.' Eddie swallows hard.

'In life, we can't control every situation we find ourselves in, no matter how much we might want to. You can't blame yourself for an accident.' Ava inches closer to

Eddie on the couch, speaking with a definite new ring of sympathy.

I can't see straight, can't think, struggling to process everything he just said. He needed that property for Matthew, but why didn't he just tell me the whole truth? I would have understood. Jesus, I would have helped him instead of fighting him.

'Why didn't he tell me?' I turn to Fran, the most sensible one out of the lot of us.

'He was ashamed. Take a look at his face. Anyone can see how badly he thinks of himself. If he can't forgive himself, how can he expect anyone else to forgive him?'

'Shhh!' Karen exclaims, pointing at the screen.

'And sorry, Eddie, but I have to ask you, what about Emma Harvey?' Ava is not quite so high on her horse now, but she won't be happy until she gets to the bottom of everything. It's the nature of the beast.

Eddie rubs his thumb under his chin again and tilts his head in question. 'Honestly?'

She nods expectantly.

He blows out a low blast of air before dropping an even bigger bomb. 'I love her.'

My stomach somersaults in an ecstatic celebratory flip.

Ava inches further forward, almost on the edge of her seat. 'You love her? After a week in Dubrovnik? Do you even know what love is?' Her features scrunch into a doubtful expression.

'Love is putting someone else's wants before your own. Love is spending a year away from them because you think they deserve better than you. Love is thinking about that person constantly, hoping they are okay, that they're happy, that they are taken care of, wishing you could be the one to do all of those things for them, but knowing you don't deserve to...'

Ava's mouth falls open in shock.

'You've known Emma Harvey for a year?' she confirms.

'Yes.' He nods. 'We met at Callum and Abby's engagement party and errr…'

I hide my face behind my hands, praying he's not going to tell the entire country I shagged him on the first night. Jesus, my mother could be watching! Not that she can say much at this stage.

'Let's just say we hit it off, as our friends had told us we would.' He recovers diplomatically, but the tiny curl of his lips assures me he remembers it as clearly as I do.

'We hit it off, and I went to the States the following day, promising to call her. But then I had the accident, and I didn't. I couldn't. I was riddled with guilt, ashamed. I couldn't stand the sight of myself. Who would want me after what I had done? I was in a bad place, I told you. She deserved so much better. She still does, but selfishly, I want her.'

'Wow. So, was the wedding the first time you saw her, after everything?' Ava's eyes glint, sensing another massive story, just not the one she'd initially been hunting down.

'We met by chance on the flight, and I was at this point, technically and publicly, very single. Things progressed anyway, as you saw for yourself in the photo.' He eyes Ava pointedly with a shrug before continuing. 'We spent the week together, and then I ruined it all again.'

'How?'

I'd nearly swear the cold-hearted ice queen Ava is almost championing us at this stage.

'It turned out that by another weird stroke of bad luck, we'd been bidding on the same Dublin property at auction. The one I bought for Matthew. She was counter-bidding on it for her new spa, her fifth branch of Believe in Beauty. I won the auction.'

'And Emma didn't take it well?'

'It's way more complicated than that. I couldn't tell her why I wanted to buy it for Matthew so badly.' I breathe out heavily. 'I couldn't tell her the rest. Not until now.'

'I'm sure nobody in this world would blame you for being the driver of that vehicle. Accidents happen every minute of every day across the world. It must have been traumatic for all of you. But it sounds like Matthew is lucky to have you,' she acknowledges, brushing her finger against the corner of her eye.

'He's not lucky, far from it. I blame myself. I wish it was me in that wheelchair. But it's not, so I have to do everything in my power to compensate my brother for that, even though it has cost me Emma, again.'

Ava pauses for a minute, seemingly stunned. 'Well...It's not what we were expecting. What about Emma? Do you think you can work it out?'

'That's up to her. I have an awful habit of breaking everything I touch. I wouldn't blame her if she wanted to give me a wide berth. Besides, she has bigger fish to fry than me. She has a baby of her own on the way.'

I smile.

'She's pregnant?' This is even more dramatic than Ava could have dreamt of. Her ratings must be reaping the rewards.

Karen gasps next to me. 'Are you...?'

I laugh and wipe a stray tear from sliding down my cheek. 'I refer to as my business as my baby.'

Eddie answers for me, all eyes trained back to the screen. 'No. She has a new business baby on the way. A brand-new cosmetics line. And if she'll let me, I am going to be the face of it, well, the face for the male cosmetics at least.'

'Well, this all sounds very intriguing. Will you join us again, Eddie? To tell us how Matthew settles in at home and reveal more about either baby, when you're able.'

'It would be my pleasure.' He extends a hand and takes Ava's.

She doesn't recoil this time.

'One more thing, Eddie,' Ava says. 'If Emma Harvey is watching this now, what do you want to tell her?'

Eddie looks directly at the camera. His eyes burn through my screen as if he can actually see me.

'I want to tell her not to get into her cab at Dublin airport. I want to tell her I'll pick her up. I want her to come home with me. I don't want to spend another second away from her.'

Ava Armstrong openly swoons, but he hasn't quite finished.

'Besides...she needs to check out the place anyway, because I've gifted it to her. I couldn't give her the house I had planned for Matthew, but I *can* give her my own. And in all honestly, it's pretty perfect for a new luxury spa, even if I do say so myself. I just hope she'll let me crash at hers until I can find something more permanent for myself.'

The tears freefall down my cheeks as the girls envelop me.

'Get off me, you big lesbos.' I swat them away as they pretend to smooch me.

CHAPTER FORTY-THREE

EDDIE

I'm back at Dublin airport, for the second time in twenty-four hours, pacing the glass tiles in the arrival area. This time I drove myself here, in the Lexus, which has been sitting pretty on my driveway for the previous year. I managed to get here in one piece, so maybe my luck is finally changing.

A crowd has gathered behind me, the power of the media, I suppose. I can't say I'm surprised. In fact, I quite like their support. I rang The Oceania as soon as I left the studio, but Emma had already checked out. I don't know if she saw my interview. If she didn't, I'm pretty sure someone will have told her about it. I can only hope she's not horrified by my confession, by the fact that it was me driving that car. I hope she understands now why I did what I did. I received a better reception than I expected from Ava Armstrong, and the entire country for that matter, so maybe, just maybe, Emma can forgive me too – forgive my dishonesty.

When the camera stopped rolling, Ava shared her own story with me. She told me she was charged with minding her little sister for the afternoon while her parents went to town for some shopping. She confessed there was a lake at the bottom of their garden. That she only took her eyes off her sister for a minute. That it was a minute more than she should have done. It seems we all have skeletons in our closets, things we aren't proud of. Apparently, they call it 'life'.

Callum's fixer came good. It cost me a substantial amount of money to obtain the Croatian medical records, but Maria's blood report revealed what I already knew. There was no trace of HCG in her blood. I await the Twitter storm of abuse from her camp, merely surprised it hasn't started already after this morning's interview with Ava.

Coach wasn't best pleased with my impromptu appearance without consulting the teams PR. For a second, I thought he might drop me from the team, but he rang to say he was proud of me and that I was a great role model for the youngsters to look up to. Mind you, with guys like Marcus running the beach naked, it's not difficult to be compared favourably at the moment. We'll see how proud he is after tomorrow's match performance.

As a new swarm of bodies begin to trickle through the arrival zone, I spot James and Nadine, followed closely by Marcus, Ollie and Nathan. It's one thing having an anonymous audience. It's an entirely different matter having the entire team here to witness my epic declaration. At least I know her flight is in.

'Harrington, you just can't stay away, can you? Did you miss me already?' Marcus bellows across like an excited baboon. Before he reaches me, he's intercepted by Shelly launching herself at him, leaping up into his arms, and simultaneously berating him for his naked viral vocal internet sensation. Those two are a match made in heaven. What you see is what you get – one louder than the other.

James approaches and extends his fist for an encouraging

pump before leading his wife towards the gathering crowd, who are now asking every member of the team they spot for an autograph.

My head jerks up, like my heart knows that she is breathing the same air as me. She wears the same dress she wore on Bob's boat, her shoulders are decidedly browner than they were this time last week, and freckles dot her make-up free face. She looks beautiful. Natural, vulnerable, yet her hard-set jaw implies she's anticipating conflict.

I watch as she takes it all in, scanning the crowd. Her feet remain rooted to the spot, white knuckles grasp the handle of her suitcase. Finally, her olive eyes meet mine, and uncertainty glints in her iris. Her free hand twists the ends of the hair that cascades loosely over her shoulders.

The intrusive flashing of cameras illuminate the room, and the previously noisy chatter has ceased to an eerie silence. The sound of my pounding heart thunders through my eardrums, my thumb automatically rubs my scar. Seconds feel like minutes as we stare at each other, locked in a silent exchange.

Can you forgive me?

Can we get through this?

Will you be mine?

Every cell inside me zings to life. This woman sets my world alight yet simultaneously soothes my soul. My need for her is comparable to nothing else. My feet make a decision of their own, powering my legs towards her, my eyes never leaving hers. She launches herself into my arms, leaping from the floor to wrap her legs around my waist. I squeeze her into me and press my face against hers.

'I'm so sorry.' I bury my face into her neck, drinking in the scent of her skin.

She tilts her head up and holds my face in her two hands

like it's a precious stone. 'Kiss me like you mean it,' she says, repeating the dare that Abby issued by the pool.

My eager lips meet her full opening mouth, her tongue slips against mine, as she presses herself firmly against me. I tighten my arms around her, protecting her, sheltering her. The crowd erupt in a thunderous stampede of clapping and whistling, but they melt away, insignificant compared to the noise of my hammering heart. I break away, reluctantly, but desperate to get her away from here and to the privacy of our own home.

'You are rocking my world.' I deliberately use the line I used on her the first night, I meant it then, and I mean it now.

'You are my world.' Her cherry lips curl upwards into a beaming smile. 'Now bring me home.'

CHAPTER FORTY-FOUR

EMMA

The player's lounge is a large rectangular room with a mahogany bar running the length of the back wall. Floor-to-ceiling glass doors open up on to an enormous exclusive outdoor seating area overlooking the pitch. It's my first time at the Aviva Stadium, but already I love it here.

I clutch a glass of chilled white wine in my right hand as Abby steers me towards the seating area outside. The match is about to start. Almost everyone important to Eddie is here, his mother, his father, his two sisters. He briefly introduced me before running off to the changing rooms to prepare. Keira repeatedly glances at me with unconcealed curiosity. I'd be curious too if I were her. Amy takes the seat on the other side of me and offers a gigantic widespread smile displaying porcelain teeth that are three shades too white to be natural.

Callum stands on edge in the commentators' box thirty feet away, wearing a crisp grey suit, clutching a microphone in his right hand. His father, Nadine and Shelly are all in attendance, along with many other faces I don't recognise. There's a distinct sense of building tension, a united desire to see our men win. I wonder if I will become a regular fixture here? I'd like to be, that's for sure.

The referee blows the whistle, and Abby clutches my clammy hand as the game begins. It appears hard, fast and vicious to my inexperienced eyes, but running commentary declares our team is slow, sluggish and in need of upping their game. Munster have the distinct advantage with the majority of possession after the first half of the game. The scoreboard reflects this – fluorescent LED lights display it's 21–18 to them.

Our boys just can't seem to take the lead, the week's debauchery possibly catching up with them. Abby fills me in on the terminology as the game unfolds. Family members dissect each move, breaking down who should have done what when. None of it matters. All that matters is that they turn it around somehow.

My heart is heavy as the second half begins just as badly. Marcus endures a cruel-looking tackle from the opposition, sending him flying four feet into the air before he lands less than graciously on his back. It looks serious from where I'm sitting, but he jumps up without complaint. James O'Malley charges at his competition head-on, retaking the ball. He dropkicks the ball from just past the halfway line resulting in a drop goal, giving everyone a much-needed sense of hope. Nadine jumps to her feet and screams her husband's name in ecstatic delight.

Leinster manage to maintain possession. Eddie glances up towards us and resumes his position in the front row of the scrum. I watch through half-closed eyelids, wincing at the brutality of the game whilst simultaneously enthralled by the power and strength of the men that play it.

Marcus travels rapidly across the pitch at an unexpected opportunity and passes the ball once again to Eddie, who takes off at full speed before leaping onto the ground and slamming the ball over the line. The crowd erupt with wild hoots and cheers, but this isn't the time to get complacent. Who will take the shot for the conversion?

The stadium falls deathly quiet as Marcus steps forward to take the shot.

Abby leans in and whispers, 'He needs this more than you know. It's the perfect chance to redeem himself after the video that went viral. Callum said Coach was livid.' Her fingers clench radiating her obvious tension. She's rooting for Marcus, not just the team.

Marcus lines the ball up to take the shot. I hang on to Abby barely breathing. Marcus's right leg swings back before powerfully smashing the ball over the bar. I scream alongside the others, leaping to my feet, hugging Eddie's family, and his teammates' family members like I've known them forever.

I always wanted a big family. Though it may be in the unlikeliest of places, it looks like I might finally have found it.

EPILOGUE

FOUR MONTHS LATER

EMMA

I pace the floor of the previously renovated extension. Thank god for it because Eddie's stuff takes up just as much space as my own. He's been living here since we got back. It made perfect sense as we've transformed his place into the luxurious spa salon I had planned. The car arrives, a black sleek Mercedes, and we slide in, on route to the long-anticipated launch.

Over three hundred guests are in attendance; vloggers, celebrities, Ava Armstrong and of course the entire rugby team. Since he returned from the States, Matthew has excelled in his new role as my business marketing manager. Almost as handsome as his younger brother, he was made to market beauty products to willing women.

We arrive to see a large crowd gathered already. Waitresses discreetly distribute crystal flutes filled with bubbling champagne. The low hum of expectant chatter charges the air. Scented Serapy candles flicker from every corner of the drawing-room. Luxurious deep-seated sofas occupy the far end of the space. I take a deep breath and scan the faces that surround me. Almost everybody important to me is already here.

Eddie stands by my side, never more than a foot away from me. He's not only my boyfriend. He's my best friend, my biggest champion and the new face of my male skincare range. The husband search is finally over. And now I've found him, I'm truly in no rush to run down that aisle, finally confident that a proposal will materialise when *he* deems the time to be right.

Matthew walks slowly towards us, supported with a stick on one side and Amy on the other. Just like me and Eddie, he continues to grow stronger each day.

Our mutual friends congregate around us; Abby, Callum, Fran, Karen and Kerry clink glasses companionably. I've never been able to ask Kerry about that night with Nathan, but if the way he's staring at her tonight is anything to go by, he's clearly not given up the chase yet.

My mother hovers awkwardly nearby scrutinising the place, with her new man in tow. She's even partially smiling, which is more than I dared to hope for. I can't forget how she treated me – her constant disapproval – but I have forgiven it. And I do sort of understand. We have an awful tendency to hurt the ones we love, so in a weird fucked-up way, I have to take her digs as a compliment. She does love me. Even if I am the image of my father, a man she wasn't ever truly happy with.

My two sisters link arms five feet away. Grace's bump protrudes in front of her, and Holly's phone beeps incessantly, no doubt more additions to her X-rated collage. Frankie sniffs the floor between my guests, perpetually hoping for a fallen pastry. I glance at the door one more time and pat my hair into place. I can't hold off much longer. I have to accept that he isn't coming. Maybe it's too much to ask him to be in the same room as her. Or maybe he's just too busy.

Sarah approaches. 'You ready, boss?'

'She was born ready.' Eddie leans in and answers for me, planting a kiss on my lips.

'Mind my lipstick.' I wink at him. I've mostly abandoned the inch-thick foundation, no longer requiring the protection of a mask, but the crimson lipstick seemed appropriate for the occasion.

'That's not what you said earlier. I have the marks to prove it,' he whispers, deliberately brushing his lips against my sensitive earlobe.

'You can do what you like with me once we get the photos for *Tattler* done.'

'I'm going to hold you to that.' He squeezes my hand and nods towards the door.

My heart leaps in my chest as my father rushes through the door, his coat buttoned up to the chin, still not yet re-acclimatised to the winter weather and the biting wind blowing in from the Irish sea. He strolls confidently through the crowd, oozing the same presence he always has, causing cameras to click as he approaches us.

'Emma.' He kisses my cheek and shakes Eddie's hand before glancing around at the interior.

'Congratulations.' He pulls me into one of those awkward dad hugs that I've missed.

'Thank you for coming.'

'Thanks for giving me the opportunity. I'm so proud of you, sweetheart.' He places an arm around my shoulder, and I find myself wedged protectively between the two most important men in my life.

Sarah hands me a microphone, and I make my way to the front of the room with Eddie closely on my heels.

'Good evening. Thank you so much for joining me on this crisp December night to launch my new spa, my fifth branch of Believe in Beauty. Even though I personally chose the name of my businesses, it took me a really long time to believe in the words themselves, to actually believe in a different type of beauty. I'm not talking about the way we look; I'm talking about having the confidence to let our inner beauty radiate from within, to have the confidence to follow our dreams, to feel that we *can* and *deserve* to achieve them.'

I pause deliberately to let my words sink in before continuing. 'But until we find that confidence, find that certainty, we can always rely on a spa day, face cream and a mask.' A chortle of laughter ripples around the room.

'For years, I've hidden behind the mask of make-up, self-conscious of my own skin. I wanted to invent a product that would replace the need to cover up my imperfections. While I was trying to find that product, I became a product myself, of something else. Thankfully, I saw the light. So here it is guys, The Serapy Skincare range, produced here in Ireland, made with Irish ingredients straight from that sea.' I point to the crashing waves outside the balcony doors.

'I hope you like it. It was made with love and a lot of heartfelt lessons.'

A rhythmic clapping drowns out everything else around me. Eddie takes my hand and raises it to the roof in victory.

It took ten years and five businesses for me to realise, I don't have to have a man to define my success. I define my own, with him by my side.

THE END

OTHER BOOKS IN THE SERIES

OTHER TITLES BY LYNDSEY GALLAGHER:

The Seven Year Itch

The Midwife Crisis

How Will I know?

ACKNOWLEDGEMENTS

Some books are easier to write than others, this one was a product of NanoWriMo (National Novel Writing Month), and it almost broke me at times. Although it was a great excuse to mentally escape to Croatia during the darkest months of the year, in the middle of the pandemic. I have an awful soft spot for Dubrovnik, having holidayed there myself, and it's top of our list for when we are allowed to travel again. Until then, thank goodness for amazing books and for my amazing husband.

As usual, I have to thank my fabulous friends, whose jobs I often 'borrow' for my characters and then proceed to wreck their heads by asking three thousand questions about said profession! Didn't get to use the waxing stories this time, Niamh, but nothing goes to waste. I'm saving them all up for a rainy day! Trina, you continue to provide me with an endless amount of laugh out loud moments which could fill a hundred books! I'm definitely going to have a teacher protagonist one day very soon!

Thank you to my writing buddies Lucy Keeling, Jenny Hickman, Emma Farrell, Margaret Amatt and Adrian Wills, who have kept me going, encouraged and supported me, and answered endless questions from the woman who is mostly winging it by the seat of her pants! Some of the most supportive people I have come across are the ones that I have yet to meet in person. I'm hoping to meet most of you one day at a writers' conference, preferably in New York with an endless supply of prosecco! Thank you to my fabulous beta readers Vikkie Wakeham and Aoife McDonagh. You'll have to come to the writing conferences too. I am so grateful to Margaret and Emma for putting me in touch with their fabulous editor Aimee Walker.

Thank you so much to all of you fabulous people that read my stories, and those that reach out to me afterwards to tell me so. It makes every single second of torturous editing worth it when I hear you have enjoyed it, so thank you.

ABOUT THE AUTHOR

Lyndsey Gallagher is an eternal sucker for a swoon-worthy, happy ever after. She lives in the west of Ireland with her husband, two children and a boxer puppy. When she's not writing, Lyndsey can be found curled up in front of the fire with a good book and a G&T.

Made in United States
North Haven, CT
12 May 2023

36500553R00152